TALES OF ETHSHAR

TALES OF ETHSHAR

LAWRENCE WATT-EVANS

TALES OF ETHSHAR

Published by Wildside Press, LLC
www.wildsidebooks.com

CONTENTS

INTRODUCTION

Ethshar?

Some readers already recognize the name, and can skip this introduction, but if you aren't one of them, perhaps a brief explanation is in order.

"Ethshar" is what we call an invented world that's been the setting for almost a dozen novels so far. Its inhabitants don't call it that; they call it "the World." For readers, though, that's not specific enough. The dominant nation on the World is the Hegemony of the Three Ethshars, while the largest, richest city, where most of the stories are set, is Ethshar of the Spices, so "Ethshar" is close enough. The name itself comes from words meaning "safe harbor."

You don't need to have read any of the novels to enjoy the stories herein; each one should stand alone. Here's a little background, though:

The World of Ethshar is rich in magic—several varieties of magic, in fact, each with its own rules, its own strengths, and its own weaknesses. In these stories you'll find wizardry, sorcery, theurgy, and warlockry, but there are others, as well.

About half the inhabited World is the Hegemony of Ethshar, ruled by the overlords of its three great cities: Ethshar of the Rocks, Ethshar of the Sands, and Ethshar of the Spices. To the north of the Hegemony lie the Tintallions, the Baronies of Sardiron, and anarchic lands like Srigmor; to the east are the Small Kingdoms, more than a hundred tiny squabbling states. To the south and west is only ocean, right to the edge of the World—yes, the World is flat and has edges. It has two moons, one pink, the other orange. The greater moon follows a thirty-day cycle much like our own moon's, while the lesser moon goes through all its phases in about a day and a half.

The people of Ethshar measure time from the year the gods first taught human beings to talk—or at least, so legend says. Much knowledge of their history was lost in the course of the Great War, a centuries-long struggle between Old Ethshar and the Northern Empire that ended, in the last decade of the fiftieth century of human speech, with the utter destruction of the Northerners.

The stories in this collection are all set at various times in the three hundred years following the Great War. Ethshar stories are generally not tales of great heroes battling evil, but of ordinary people trying to deal with an extraordinary world.

The novels, in order of publication (which is *not* the order of their events), are these:

The Misenchanted Sword
With A Single Spell
The Unwilling Warlord
The Blood of a Dragon
Taking Flight
The Spell of the Black Dagger
Night of Madness
Ithanalin's Restoration
The Spriggan Mirror
The Vondish Ambassador
The Unwelcome Warlock

I have hopes of writing several more. Meanwhile, I hope you'll enjoy these little stories!

ABOUT "THE BLOODSTONE"

In The Misenchanted Sword, *the very first published Ethshar story, I referred to "the bloodstone spell" that allowed the soldiers of the Holy Kingdom of Ethshar to survive for extended periods without food. I was well aware that such a spell deserved more than a passing mention, and eventually I wrote this story about it.*

THE BLOODSTONE

Darranacy wrinkled her nose in disgust at the smell from Mama Kilina's cookpot. "What *is* that?" she asked.

"Cabbage, mostly," Mama Kilina replied, poking at a whitish lump. "Cabbage someone pickier than me thought was too far gone to eat."

"Whoever it was that threw it out wouldn't get any argument from me!" Darranacy retorted, turning away.

Kilina looked up at her. "Oh, and I suppose you'd eat it if it were fresh? Some of us don't have your advantages, my girl! We take what we can get!"

Darranacy smiled smugly. "One of us doesn't have to."

Kilina glared at her for a moment, then went back to her stew. "Laugh while you can, girl," she said. "Someday the spell will break, and when it does you'll be in the same boat as the rest of us."

"Or maybe someday you'll *wish* it was broken," a voice said from behind, startling Darranacy so that she jumped. She turned and found a smiling young man dressed in tattered red velvet.

"Korun!" she said. "Don't sneak up on me like that!"

"Learn to listen, then," he said.

Darranacy frowned slightly. "I don't understand how you can hear so much in a place like this," she said, waving her hand to take in all of Wall Street and the Wall Street Field, the run-down houses, the city wall, and the dozens of ragged figures huddled around campfires or under blankets in between. "It's not as if we were out in the forest, where it's quiet."

"You haven't learned to listen," Korun said mildly.

"I *do* listen!" she protested.

"Do you? Then what was it I said that startled you so, just now?"

"You said I should learn to listen, of course!"

"No," Korun corrected her, "That was the *second* thing I said, *after* I had startled you and you had told me not to sneak up on you."

Darranacy opened her mouth to argue, then closed it again.

He was right, of course. It would hardly have made sense otherwise.

But then what *had* he said?

"Oh, I don't know!" she snapped. "I was too startled to listen to the words!"

"I said," Korun told her, "that someday you may wish that your magic spell was broken."

"Oh, that was it." She frowned. "But what a silly thing to say, Korun. Why would I ever wish that?" Before he could answer, she continued, "And if I did, the spell is very easy to break—the hard part is *keeping* it. If I let the enchanted bloodstone out of my possession, the spell will fade away, or if any food or water passes my lips, poof! The spell's gone. I could break it right now with a single bite of Mama Kilina's glop—if I wanted to, which I most certainly don't." She shuddered at the very idea. She missed the taste of food, sometimes, but that stuff didn't really qualify.

"I have heard," Korun said, "that it is unwise to maintain the spell for too long. Magic always has a cost, Darra. An old wizard once told me that the bloodstone spell can wear you down and damage your health."

"Damage my health, ha!" Darranacy replied. "If I wanted to damage my health, all I would have to do is eat some of the stuff you people live on. The Spell of Sustenance can't be any worse for me than that cabbage. I haven't eaten a bite nor drunk a drop in four months now, and I'm just as fit as ever."

Korun shrugged. "I say what I heard, that's all."

"You're just jealous because *you* have to eat," the girl said. "You spend your time scrounging for hand-outs, and any money you get goes for food and drink, and you'll probably be here on Wall Street for the rest of your life, but I don't need *anything*. I'm free!"

Mama Kilina looked up. "'Tain't natural, living like that."

"Of course it isn't natural," Darranacy answered promptly. "It's magic!"

Mama Kilina just shook her head and went back to her cookery.

"You're right, of course," Korun said. "It *is* magic, and it gives you an advantage over the rest of us, since you don't need to worry about your next meal. But have you done much with that advantage? It doesn't appear to me that you have. You're still here in the Field, and it's been, as you say, four months since your parents died."

"There's no hurry," Darranacy said defensively. "I'm still young."

"Ah, but wouldn't it be wise to use your advantage and get yourself out of here while you *are* still young?"

"I *will* get out of here!" Darranacy shouted. "And I'll *stay* out!"

"When?"

"When I'm old enough for an apprenticeship! When I'm good and ready!"

Korun shook his head. "I don't think," he said, "that this is quite what old Naral had in mind when he put the spell on you."

"Who cares what old Naral thinks?"

"*You* ought to, girl," Mama Kilina snapped. "Without him, you'd be no better off than any of us. If your mother hadn't been his apprentice once, and if he hadn't felt guilty when one of the spells he had taught her went wrong, you'd be starving now."

"No, I wouldn't," Darranacy retorted, "because if Mother had never been his apprentice, she wouldn't have had any spells to go wrong, and she'd still be alive!"

"No, she wouldn't," Kilina insisted, "because it wasn't her spell that killed her, as you well know, it was the demon your father summoned. Bad luck, mixing two schools of magic in a marriage like that, that's what *I* say."

"But if she hadn't been a wizard, she would have run, instead of trying to stop the demon from taking Daddy—if she'd ever have married a demonologist in the first place."

Kilina shook her head. "Wizard or no, and whatever else, your mother probably wouldn't have left your father if all the demons of Hell were after him."

Darranacy opened her mouth, and then closed it again. She couldn't think of any way to argue with that. Should she insist that her mother would have fled, she'd be denying her parents' love for each other.

Why did they have to die, anyway? Why did magic have to be so dangerous?

"Oh, it doesn't matter," she said at last. "They're both dead, and Naral *did* give me the bloodstone."

"Yes," Korun said, "He gave you the stone and the spell, and he told you that that was all he could do, to let you get by until you could find a place for yourself."

"Well, then?" Darranacy snapped.

"Darra," Korun said quietly, "I think he had four *days* in mind, maybe as much as four *sixnights*, but not four *months*—or four *years*, the way you've been going."

"*Three* years. I'll be twelve in less than three years, and then I'll find an apprenticeship."

"You plan to stay that long? To keep the spell that long?"

"Why not?" Darranacy stared up at him.

"Do you think you'll be in any shape to serve an apprenticeship after three years here?"

"Why not?" Darranacy asked again.

Korun didn't answer.

He didn't have to.

Naral hadn't mentioned anything about the bloodstone's spell being unhealthy; Darranacy was sure that Korun was just jealous when he said that.

But even so, what would she have to wear after three years in the Field? She'd have outgrown all her clothes, and would just have rags. Who would she know who could give her a reference? What sort of diseases might she have caught? The bloodstone didn't keep away disease. Or fleas, or lice, or ringworm, or any number of other things that might deter a prospective master.

Magic always seemed to have these little tricks and loopholes built into it—but then, so did everything else in life. Nothing was ever as simple as she wanted it to be.

"All right, then, I'll find a place sooner!" she said. "I'll fix myself up and I'll be in fine shape when I turn twelve!"

Korun smiled sadly.

"You think I *won't* find a place for myself?" she demanded.

"I think you won't unless you start looking," Korun told her. "I've seen too many people start out with fine plans and high hopes only to rot here in the Wall Street Field. You think Mama Kilina, here, never set her sights any higher than this?"

Darranacy turned and started to say something rude, then stopped.

She had never thought of Mama Kilina ever being anywhere else. Just days after the demon had carried her parents off, leaving their tidy little apartment and shop a burnt-out ruin, and after Naral had enchanted her but refused to take her in, the tax collector had come around for the annual payment on the family's property.

Darranacy hadn't had the payment—she hadn't had any money at all, had never found where her parents had hidden their savings, if in fact they had any. She had packed up a few belongings and fled, crying, and had come to the Field—everyone in Ethshar of the Sands knew that that was the last refuge, the place where the city guard never bothered you and nobody cared who you were or what you'd done. She'd found Mama Kilina there, sitting by her cooking pot, just as she was now, and it had never occurred to her, then or any time since, to wonder how old Kilina came there.

Even Kilina must have been young once, though.

Mama Kilina grinned at her. She still had almost half her teeth, Darranacy saw.

Darranacy did not want to ever wind up like Mama Kilina, bent and old and eating rotten cabbage.

"All right," Darranacy said, "I'll *find* a place, then. Right now!"

"How?" Korun asked quietly.

Darranacy looked up at him angrily. "Why should I tell you?" she demanded, as she stared challengingly at Korun.

He shrugged. "Please yourself, child," he said. He squatted down by the cookpot. "Spare me a little, Mama?"

Darranacy watched as the two of them ate Mama Kilina's cabbage stew. The smell reached her, and simultaneously revolted and enticed her.

She never felt real hunger now, but the smell of food could still affect her—even such food as this. She remembered the happy meals with her parents in the back of the shop, the pastries her father sometimes bought her when they were out on one errand or another, how she would sit and nibble at a bowl of salted nuts while she practiced her reading...

But she couldn't eat anything now. It would break the spell, and then she'd need to find more food or starve, she'd need to find clean water—the stuff the others here in the Field drank, mostly rainwater collected from gutters of the city ramparts or from gravel-lined pits dug in the mud, was foul and full of disease. Attempts to dig a proper well had always been stopped by the city guard—the edict that had created the Field in the first place said that no permanent structure was permitted between

Wall Street and the city wall itself, and that included wells as well as buildings.

Once she had a proper home again, *then* she could break the spell. Not before.

She thought over Korun's words. He was right, it was time to find a proper home.

She stood up and turned away from Mama Kilina and her cookpot, and began walking.

Darranacy reached her own little shelter, built of sticks and knotted-together rags pilfered from Grandgate Market—a crude thing that could be knocked down, or simply trampled, in a matter of seconds if the city guard ever decided to clear the Field out properly. She ducked inside, shoved aside her crude bedding, and dug into the sand, uncovering the pack she had hidden there.

This pack held everything she had brought from her parents' house that she wasn't already wearing.

There wasn't anything really valuable in the pack; the demon and the fire had destroyed all her parents' precious arcane supplies, the dragon's blood and virgin's tears and so on that her mother had used, and Darranacy hadn't been able to find any gold or silver anywhere—maybe the demon had taken it all, some demons did crave money, though her father had never told her what they did with it.

There was, however, her good tunic—fine brown silk with elaborate rucking around the waist, and gold embroidery on the sleeves and hem. Wearing that she would be attired well enough to travel anywhere in the city, up to and including the Palace itself.

She looked down at it for a moment.

She could go anywhere in it—but where should she go?

She wasn't about to go to the Palace; that was too much. The overlord scared her; she'd never met him, but she had heard enough about him that she was not about to intrude on the Palace.

But she wanted to find someone rich to live with.

Well, there were plenty of big, elaborate homes *around* the Palace, homes where rich people lived. She didn't know how she could get someone there to take her in, but maybe if she looked around…

An hour later Darranacy, in her fine silk tunic but still barefoot, was wandering the streets of the Morningside district, admiring the marble shrines on the street corners, the iron fences and ornate gates that guarded the homes, the lush gardens behind the fences, the lavish homes beyond the gardens.

This was so different from the crowded streets where she had always lived! On Wizard Street or Wall Street the shops were jammed against each other right along the street, with no room for gardens either between them or in front of them, and the courtyards to the rear would hold only small vegetable patches, not these great expanses of flowers in every color of the rainbow. The residents lived upstairs from their shops, or behind them—a home without a business, a building without a signboard over the door or a display in the window, was rare indeed. A block a hundred yards long would hold at least a dozen homes in a solid row, broken perhaps by a single dark, narrow alley—two at the most.

Here, such a block would have but two or three houses, each standing apart amid its own gardens and terraces, closed off from the street and its neighbors by walls and fences—if there *were* businesses in there, customers had no way in! Windows gleamed on every side, fountains splashed—Darranacy couldn't quite imagine living amid such sybaritic surroundings.

And there didn't seem to be all that many people who actually *did* live there. She saw a young couple on a bench in one garden, and a woman tending flowers in another, but for the most part the yards were empty, the streets almost deserted.

Darranacy guessed that there weren't enough rich people to fill all those big houses, and that encouraged her—they must be lonely, in there.

But she couldn't just walk in somewhere and ask to be adopted.

She walked on, and saw three little children, all of them much younger than herself, playing ball on the terrace of a particularly fine mansion.

A boy of seven or so was climbing a tree a few doors down, and she considered calling out to him, but decided not to.

She was almost to Smallgate Street, and the houses were growing smaller and squeezing in four to the block, when she saw the girl.

She wasn't playing, or climbing, or gardening; she was just standing there, leaning on a fence, her face thrust between the iron bars, looking out at the world beyond her home. She was taller than Darranacy, and probably older, but she wore just a tunic, not a dress but a dark red tunic with no skirt, which meant she was still a child, not yet twelve—or if her parents were exceptionally old-fashioned, it meant she hadn't had her first monthly flow yet.

"Hi," Darranacy said, from a few steps away.

The girl blinked at her. "Hello," she said back.

"My name's Darranacy."

"I'm Shala."

"You live here?"

Shala nodded.

"You look bored."

"I am."

"So am I," Darranacy lied.

"Want to do something together?"

Darranacy almost gasped with relief.

"Sure," she said.

"Come on in," Shala said, pointing to the gate.

This was the perfect opportunity. Darranacy hurried into the yard.

Now, how could she bring up the idea of adoption?

She thought about that as Shala took her inside and found a pair of dolls, as Shala introduced her to her mother and the housekeeper, as they went back outside and played out game after game...but as time passed, she thought about it less and less. She was having too much fun.

The two girls played princess-and-hero with the dolls, and romantic rivals (a stick served as the object of their competing affections), and various other games—but Shala balked when Darranacy suggested playing wizards.

"My Dad doesn't like magic," she said. "He says it makes people lazy and careless—they figure if anything goes wrong, magic can fix it."

Darranacy blinked in surprise. "But magic's *hard*," she said. "And dangerous and expensive. You don't use it for stuff where you don't have to."

"*Some* people do, my Dad says," Shala said darkly. "He talks about that a lot—he says the overlord depends on magic more than he ought to, and since he's the overlord, it doesn't matter how hard or dangerous or expensive it is."

"But..." Darranacy began.

Then she stopped.

If Shala's father didn't like magic, then she was in the wrong place. Both her parents had been magicians, after all, and she was proud of that—even if it *had* gotten them killed in the end.

Magic was hard and dangerous, and shouldn't be used if you didn't need it, but there wasn't anything *wrong* with it.

If there were...well, right now her whole *life* depended on magic. Without her enchanted bloodstone she'd be a beggar starving in the Wall Street Field, instead of...

Well, so she *was* a beggar living in the Wall Street Field, but she wasn't *starving*, and she wasn't going to stay there.

"Come on," Shala said, "we can have your doll be an evil magician, and *my* doll will be a hero who has to kill her without getting turned into a newt or something."

"Okay," Darranacy said, a bit reluctantly. "What kind of magician? A sorcerer?"

"What's that?"

Darranacy blinked, and struggled for an explanation. Her parents had taught her the differences among all the various schools of magic, but that didn't mean she could explain them to Shala.

"How about a magician who can call up demons for my doll to fight?" Shala asked.

"A demonologist?" Darranacy said. "But they're not really evil, they just have a bad reputation." She saw Shala's expression, and quickly amended that. "At least, my father always said *some* of them weren't evil."

Before Shala could reply, the housekeeper's voice called her name from the back door.

"It must be dinner time," Shala said. "Do you want to eat dinner with us? Would your parents mind?"

This was her chance, Darranacy realized. If she were going to say anything, learn anything useful from Shala, this would be the time.

"I don't have any parents," she said.

Shala blinked.

"They're dead," Darranacy continued.

"Oh, Darra, I'm sorry! So do you live with your grandparents, or something?"

Darranacy shook her head. "No," she said. "I live by myself. In fact, I was here today looking for someone who might adopt me."

"Oh!" Shala stared at her.

"Shala of Morningside, get in here!" Shala's mother called from the door.

"I have to go—Darra, come on in! I'd love it if you could stay here—maybe not permanently, but maybe you could stay for a little while? I bet my Dad could find a place for you!" Shala grabbed Darranacy's hand and began tugging her toward the house.

Darranacy came reluctantly. Now that she finally had the chance, she was losing her nerve. This wasn't the right place, with a father who hated magic, and this big strange house—but it might be the only chance she would get.

At the door Shala announced loudly, "This is my friend Darra—can she stay for dinner?"

"No, I can't," Darranacy said quickly, even though the mouth-watering smells of roast beef and fresh-baked bread were incredibly, unbearably tempting.

But she couldn't eat anything, or the spell would be broken and she would starve.

"Hello, Darra," Shala's mother said. "I saw you two playing so nicely out there—we'd be pleased if you stayed." She gestured at the dining table.

"No," Darranacy said weakly. "Thank you."

She stared at the lavish meal that was set out—sliced roast beef and several different vegetables and hot buttered bread, steaming on the table.

It had been so long since she had eaten anything, and there was so *much* here, and it looked so *good!* This wasn't the mess in Mama Kilina's stewpot, this was *real* food.

Korun was almost right after all, she thought—right now she *almost* wished she didn't have the spell on her.

But she *needed* the spell. She couldn't trust these people, they wouldn't want to keep the daughter of two magicians, and when they threw her out with her magic gone she'd have nothing left at all, she'd starve in the Wall Street Field.

This might be her chance to find a home—but it was too much to risk.

"Thank you for inviting me," she said politely, "but I really can't stay."

"But Darra, you said you didn't have any family!" Shala protested. "Why can't you stay?"

Darranacy looked at Shala, and at her mother, and her father, and the housekeeper, all of them standing around the table and staring at their ungrateful guest. She patted the purse on her belt and felt the reassuring shape of the bloodstone.

"I just can't," she said. Her eyes felt hot and her throat thick, as if she were about to start crying.

"Well, all right," Shala's mother said. "If you can't stay, you can't, but we won't let you go away empty-handed." She picked up something from the table, and stepped over closer to Darranacy.

"Here," she said, "just a little something."

And as Darranacy started to refuse, Shala's mother popped a candy into Darranacy's mouth.

Darranacy froze, then started to spit the candy out, then stopped.

It was too late; she could feel it. The spell was broken, and her empty stomach growled, for the first time in four months.

And then she *did* start weeping, sobbing hysterically as she collapsed in a heap on the floor.

Shala's entire family rushed to comfort her. It took twenty minutes before she had calmed down enough to make a clear explanation, and the food was cold when the five of them finally ate, but it was still the best dinner Darranacy had ever had.

She stayed three years.

And when the time came she was not apprenticed to a wizard, nor a demonologist, nor any other magician, but instead, at her own request, to a cook. The bloodstone, no longer enchanted, paid for her apprenticeship fee.

Cookery was a magic she could *trust*.

ABOUT "INGREDIENTS"

Given the workings of wizardry as I described it in all the stories, it was clear that finding the ingredients for one's spells might be the hardest part of the entire spell-working process. That was an obvious source of stories. I also wanted to give readers a glimpse of the political situation in the Kingdoms of Tintallion. This tale was the result.

INGREDIENTS

Irillon watched, fascinated and appalled, as Therindallo was dragged up onto the scaffold. He wasn't struggling, but that was obviously because he had already been severely beaten; his hair was matted with blood.

She frowned at that—partly from her natural human sympathy, but also wondering whether that might cause her any difficulty. She needed both blood and hair, but they were supposed to be separate—and she was fairly sure she needed the blood to be liquid, not clotted.

Finding herself thinking so callously about human blood troubled her. There were times, ever since she began her apprenticeship, when she had serious reservations about this whole wizardry business, and this was one of those times. In fact, this was perhaps the most extreme yet. She had always known that wizards required a variety of odd ingredients for their spells, and even that some of them were not just odd but loathsome, but until now she had not really given much thought to just what that meant—not until her master, Ethtallion the Mage, had told her what she was to fetch this time.

In the past eighteen months since becoming Ethtallion's apprentice she had gathered ash from the hearth, had helped catch spiders, had ground up those spiders once they were properly dried out, had bought roosters' toes from the local farmers, had collected her own tears and drawn her own blood when asked, and none of that had been especially unpleasant—not that drawing blood had been *fun*, but it was not really dreadful.

Collecting the blood and hair of an executed criminal, and a piece of the scaffold he died on, was an entirely different matter—especially since the "criminal" in question was being beheaded for a crime Irillon herself was equally guilty of. Therindallo's "treason" was swearing fealty to the King of the Isle, rather than the King of the Coast, and Irillon of the Isle, like all her family, also took the Islander side in Tintallion's civil war.

She could hardly admit that here in the royal seat of Tintallion of the Coast, though—she would be arrested immediately, or perhaps simply killed on the spot. At the thought she glanced nervously at her neighbors in the small, sullen crowd gathered in the plaza below the walls of Coast Castle.

They didn't look very enthusiastic about the proceedings—but they were making no move to protest, either; the only visible movements were stamping and huddling against the cold. Irillon pulled her own cloak tight, and suddenly found herself shivering uncontrollably. She turned her attention back to the scaffold, trying to distract herself.

The guardsmen threw Therindallo on the block and buckled a strap across his shoulders; the executioner stepped forward and raised his axe. Then he paused, waiting, for no reason Irillon could see.

An official in royal livery stepped forward, fumbling with his coat; he pulled out a paper and began to read aloud.

It was a short speech that basically said King Serulinor was the rightful ruler of Tintallion and that he was having Therindallo's head chopped off for not agreeing. A good many words were wasted reciting Serulinor's alleged titles and grievances, and rejecting his cousin's claim to the throne; Irillon's attention wandered, and she found herself glancing up at the overcast sky, wondering whether it was going to snow again.

She hoped not; she had walked almost ten leagues through the snow to get here, and the walk back would be quite bad enough without the weather gods adding any further depth to what was already on the ground.

Then the official finished reading, rolled up his message, and tucked it in his sleeve, and the executioner's axe fell without any further ceremony, so suddenly that Irillon didn't quite see it happen.

Blood splashed, a really amazing quantity of blood, and Therindallo's head dropped into the waiting basket. The executioner knew his job, and had needed only a single stroke.

Gasps and a smothered squeal came from the audience. Irillon gagged at the sight of the headless body, then swallowed hard, trying to tell herself that at least it was quick, and Therindallo couldn't have suffered much. It was over—and now she needed to get Therindallo's blood and hair, and a piece of the scaffold.

Two of the guards were dragging the body away, though, and a third followed, carrying the basket. The executioner was climbing down one set of steps, the official down the other, and the little crowd was already dispersing.

Irillon blinked in surprise and almost called out; she had somehow assumed that the body would be left there, where she could reach it. She hesitated, trying to think what she should do, and a moment later she was standing alone in the plaza, her feet sinking in muddy slush.

The scaffold was still there, at any rate; she finally collected her wits sufficiently to walk up to it, draw her belt knife, and pry a few splinters from the edge of the platform.

She looked over at the bloodstains that spread out from the block, and hurried around to the side, fishing a vial from her belt-pouch. There she stooped and peered underneath.

Yes! Blood was still dripping through the cracks between planks. She collected several drops, then sealed the vial and tucked it away. For good measure she pried up a few more splinters, this time choosing damp, stained ones.

"*Hai!*" a man's voice shouted. "Get away from there!" He spoke with a Coastal accent.

Irillon looked up, startled, and saw a guard coming toward her, one hand reaching to grab. She turned and ran, heedless of direction, out of the plaza and into the narrow ways of the surrounding town. She heard a few heavy footsteps behind her at first, but after a moment's desperate flight through the winding streets she paused, back pressed against a cold stone wall, looking and listening, and could make out no signs of pursuit.

She was panting from fear and exertion, and she gasped and swallowed, trying to catch her breath. Then she looked down at her hands.

Her knife—her *athame*, her wizard's dagger—was in one hand; the other clutched a little bundle of bloody splinters. A vial half-full of Therindallo's blood was in her pouch.

That was two of the three ingredients she had come for; now she needed some of his hair.

But the guards had taken Therindallo's head away with them, in that basket—how could she ever find it, to cut a lock of hair? She could scarcely walk openly into the castle looking for it; she was an Islander, and if the guards questioned her her accent would almost certainly give her away—she could try to disguise it, but she doubted her ability to convince anyone.

And if she were recognized as an Islander, she would get much *too* close a look at that scaffold.

It was such a shame that the king's father had been a twin, and that the wetnurse had lost track of which boy was the older; if that hadn't happened this stupid war would never have begun, and Irillon could have gone anywhere in Tintallion in relative safety. If only the Coastal King's line would die out, so the rightful king could assert his authority…

But that wasn't going to happen. Serulinor had a daughter. No son as yet, but a daughter would do to continue the feud. And Buramikin had a son, so the Islander line would also last at least another generation.

And people like Irillon would have to choose one side, and be in constant danger from the other any time they left their homes.

She had caught her breath now; she sheathed her knife, and wrapped the splinters in a handkerchief before tucking them away in her pouch.

That severed head was somewhere back in the castle. She had to go back. She couldn't go back to Ethtallion without that hair! He had already complained bitterly about her ineptitude, cursing his decision to take her on as an apprentice; if she went home without what he had sent her for he might well cast her out completely.

And while she did already know seven spells, she couldn't imagine making a living from those seven. The only one that had any obvious commercial value was the Dismal Itch, and an entire career of imposing and removing such a trivial curse had no appeal at all.

She adjusted her scarf, turning it over in hopes the guard who had chased her off wouldn't recognize her, and slogged back toward the plaza.

At least Tintallion of the Coast wasn't big enough to get really lost in, as she had on her one visit to Ethshar of the Rocks—she could catch a glimpse of the castle's central tower from almost any intersection, and use that as a guide. She arrived safely back at the square without incident.

Four big men were tearing down the scaffold; if she had waited any longer than she had she would never have been able to get a piece of it. She let her breath out in a cloud at the sight.

Then she looked at the castle, trying to imagine how she might get in. The gates, twenty feet to the right of the vanishing scaffold, were closed, the portcullis down. The walls were cold, featureless stone, thirty feet high, topped with elaborate battlements…

And on those battlements two soldiers were setting a pike into place, with Therindallo's head impaled upon the pike.

Irillon had heard of people putting heads on pikes as a warning to others, but she had never seen it done before; she blinked, and swallowed bile.

It was truly disgusting. Therindallo's mouth hung hideously open, and something dark was oozing down the pikeshaft.

On the other hand, now she knew where she could get the hair she needed. She even knew how. The pike was set leaning out over the castle wall, for better display—all she needed to do was stand directly below it, then use Tracel's Levitation to rise straight up until she could reach out and cut a lock of hair.

But she would, of course, have to wait until the guards left. She leaned back against the wooden corner of a nearby shop, rubbing her hands together to warm them, and watched.

The pike was in place and left unattended within a minute or two; the scaffold was cleared away in perhaps a quarter of an hour. The guards ambled away—except for one, who stood by the gate, looking bored.

Irillon frowned, shuffling her feet to warm them and clear away the slush; was he going to stay there?

Apparently he was. She watched, shivering, hoping he would doze off, or step away for a moment.

If he did step away, she realized, he might not be gone for long. She would need to act quickly when the opportunity arose. Tracel's Levitation took four or five minutes to prepare—she couldn't afford to waste a second.

She opened her pouch and rummaged through it. She had brought the ingredients for all the spells she knew—tannis root for the Dismal Itch, dust for Felshen's First Hypnotic Spell, a whistle and tiny tray for the Spell of Prismatic Pyrotechnics, and so on. For the Levitation she needed a rooster's toe, an empty vial, a raindrop caught in mid-air, and her *athame*. She found them all, then stuffed everything else back.

Someone brushed past her, bundled up against the cold, and hurried across the plaza. That reminded her that it wasn't just the guard she needed to avoid; it was *anyone* in this hostile town. Fortunately, the gloomy cold and damp seemed to be keeping almost everyone inside.

With the ingredients in her hand she watched the guard; he didn't seem to have noticed her presence at all. He was staring dully straight ahead, at the next street over from the corner where she stood.

All the same, she decided she had stood in one place long enough; it might be suspicious, and besides, the cold wasn't as bad when she was moving. She began strolling along, looking in the shop windows, as if she were simply bored.

She was actually watching the reflections in the windows more than looking at the goods displayed, but she hoped no one would notice.

She had been wandering aimlessly back and forth, staying always in sight of the gate and its guard, for what seemed like hours, when at last the guard shifted uneasily, turned, and trotted out of sight down an alley, one hand tugging at his kilt.

Irillon dashed across the square, her hands already busy with the spell's preparatory gestures. She mumbled the incantation quickly as she ran.

She came to a stop with her nose to the castle wall, beside the gate and below the pike, still chanting. She dipped the raindrop up with the cock's toe, performed the necessary ritual gestures, transferred the drop to the empty vial, then closed the vial and tapped it with her *athame*.

At that tap she felt suddenly light; she tucked everything but her knife away and spoke the final word, and rose from the muddy ground.

A moment later she stopped herself, hanging unsupported thirty feet in the air, just a foot or two from poor Therindallo's ruined face. He looked much worse close up, but she refused to let herself think about that as she grabbed a hank of his hair and began sawing it free.

Seconds later, with her knife sheathed and the hair safely stuffed into yet another vial, she spoke the word that would trigger her descent.

Only then did she remember to look down.

The guard was back at his post, but now he had his sword drawn and was staring up at her.

There was nothing she could do, though; she was sinking slowly downward, like a pebble in oil, and there was no way to restore the spell before she touched ground.

Desperately, she drew her knife again and tried to think what she could do.

She was a girl of fourteen, not large for her age, armed with a belt-knife; he was a burly guardsman with a sword. She couldn't fight him fairly.

She was a wizard's apprentice, and knew just seven spells. She couldn't use Tracel's Levitation again in time to be any help; the Dismal Itch would just annoy him; and Fendel's Elementary Protection wouldn't stop cold iron, such as a sword. The Spell of Prismatic Pyrotechnics or the Sanguinary Deception or the Spell of the Spinning Coin wouldn't do any good here at all.

That left Felshen's First Hypnotic as her only chance; if she could daze the guard with it she might be able to escape before he recovered. She reached for her pouch…

But not in time; the guardsman stepped forward and grabbed her ankle before she could get the flap open. She yelped, startled, and tried to wrench free, but could not escape, and as the Levitation continued to fade she tumbled backward until she was lying on her back in the snow, one leg raised, the guardsman gripping the ankle tightly with one hand, and pointing his sword at her chest with the other.

"I think you need to speak to the Captain," the guard said, not unkindly.

Irillon, flustered but not so distraught as to forget her Islander accent, didn't reply at all.

A few moments later she was inside the castle, being escorted into a small, wonderfully warm room; guardsmen gripped both her arms, and her knife had been carefully taken away. A fire burned cheerily on the hearth at one end of the room, while armor and weapons adorned the other walls. Much of the floor-space was taken up by a heavy wooden table, its surface strewn with rolls of paper; on the far side of that table sat another guardsman, but this one was older and more elegantly attired, with rings on his fingers and a golden band about his right arm.

He looked up. "What's this?" he asked.

The right-hand guard explained, "She was stealing hair from the piked head over the gate. She flew up there and back."

The seated guardsman leaned back in his chair. "Flew?"

"Yes, sir," the guard replied.

"Just the hair? Not the whole head?"

"Just hair."

"Then she's not a relative trying to give it a proper pyre."

The guard shrugged.

The seated man looked Irillon in the eye. "I'm Captain Alderamon," he said. "Who are you?"

Irillon swallowed and said nothing.

Alderamon waited a moment, giving her time to change her mind, then sighed.

"You're a thief," he said. "Thieves we punish. If you flew, though, you might be a magician, and magicians we treat more respectfully. Now, thieves might be mute, I suppose, or deaf, but a wizard or a theurgist or a demonologist can't be, because then he couldn't recite incantations. I don't know for certain about witches or warlocks, or all the other sorts of magician, but I never *met* one who couldn't speak. Let me ask again—who are you?"

She looked at him, at his unyielding face, and realized that if she remained silent she would be treated as a common thief. While that would probably mean flogging or imprisonment rather than beheading, it still wasn't anything she cared to experience. Islander accent or not, she had to speak.

"I'm Irillon of…Irillon the Apprentice," she said, trying to imitate the captain's accent.

"Apprentice what? Who's your master?"

"Apprentice to Ethtallion the Mage. I'm a wizard."

"I thought so. Only a wizard would have any immediate use for a dead man's hair." He leaned forward, elbows on the table. "Well, Irillon, we don't want any trouble with the Wizards' Guild, but you *were* caught stealing. Can you *prove* you're a wizard's apprentice?"

"Yes," Irillon said. "If you give me back my knife I can show you a spell. And there's a spell on me that will tell my master if I'm harmed…"

"The Spell of the Spinning Coin, I suppose?" Alderamon interrupted.

"Yes," Irillon admitted, startled that a non-wizard had ever heard of it. She had certainly never heard of it before her apprenticeship.

"So if your heart stops, the coin will stop spinning. I've had it explained to me before. We certainly don't want *that*. Now, what spell can you demonstrate? Something harmless, please!"

"Ah…the Spell of Prismatic Pyrotechnics?"

Alderamon nodded, and a moment later Irillon had the spell ready. She blew on the silver whistle, and a shower of sparks in a hundred different hues sprang up from the little silver tray, exploding in tiny bursts of color.

"Very pretty," Alderamon acknowledged. "It would seem you are indeed a wizard's apprentice. Now, in that case, why were you stealing that hair, rather than buying it?"

Irillon blinked in surprise.

"*Buying* it?" she said.

"Of course."

"Ethtallion…my master just said to fetch the ingredients…"

"And he didn't mention that we sell them?" Alderamon sighed. "Well, we do. I told you, we don't want any trouble with the Wizards' Guild. That means we don't try to withhold ingredients wizards need for their spells—but that doesn't mean we'll just give them away! You don't give away your spells, do you?"

Irillon stared at him in amazed silence.

"Wizardry has been around for centuries, Irillon," the captain said. "In all that time, naturally we've found arrangements that are comfortable for everyone. What sort of fools would we be if we didn't know wizards use hair and blood and bone, and pieces of scaffold, and fireplace ash, and dragon's scales, and a thousand other things? And what would be gained by either denying wizards those ingredients, or giving them away for free?"

Irillon still couldn't think of anything to say.

"Now, do you have coins, or will we need to work out an exchange?"

"Uh…how much…I have some…"

And the dickering began.

In the end, Irillon paid seven bits in silver—all she had with her—and placed the Dismal Itch on two guardsmen who had been involved in a drunken brawl, promising to remove it again in three days. In exchange, she kept the blood, hair, and splinters she had already collected, and was allowed to depart freely.

Captain Alderamon escorted her to the castle gate. There he patted her on the shoulder and said quietly, "Here you go, girl, safe and sound—but take my advice and don't come back here. I told you we didn't want any trouble with the Wizards' Guild, and we don't, but next time might be different. Don't come here again."

Irillon, greatly relieved that her mission appeared to be a success and made bold thereby, looked up at him. "Why not?" she asked.

Alderamon grimaced. "Do you really need to ask? Your imitation of a Coastal accent is *terrible*."

Then he pushed her out the gate and turned away.

ABOUT "SIRINITA'S DRAGON"

I was invited to contribute a story to an anthology called The Ultimate Dragon. *I saw no reason it shouldn't be an Ethshar story, and something other than the standard hero-slays-dragon piece. I had previously mentioned wealthy Ethsharites keeping baby dragons as pets, and babies grow up, so what happened to those pets? Sirinita finds out.*

SIRINITA'S DRAGON

"You're going to *kill* him?" Sirinita said, staring at her mother in disbelief.

Sensella of Seagate looked at her daughter with surprised annoyance.

"Well, of *course* we're going to kill it," she said. "What else could we do? In a few sixnights it'll be eating us out of house and home—and in a year or two it might very well eat *us*. Just *look* how big it's getting!"

Sirinita looked.

She had to admit, Tharn *was* getting large. When he had first hatched she could sit him on her shoulder, with his tail around her neck, and almost forget he was there; now she could barely pick him up with both hands, and he certainly didn't fit on her shoulders.

And he *did* eat a lot.

"Really, Sirinita," her mother said, "you didn't think we could keep a full-grown dragon around the house, did you?"

"No," Sirinita admitted, "but I thought you could just let him go, somewhere outside the walls—I didn't know you were going to *kill* him!"

"Now, you ought to know better than that," Sensella said. "If we turned it loose it would eat people's livestock—and that's assuming it didn't eat *people*. Dragons are *dangerous*, honey."

"*Tharn* isn't!"

"But it *will* be." Sensella hesitated, then added, "Besides, we can sell the blood and hide to wizards. I understand it's quite valuable."

"Sell *pieces* of him?" This was too much; Sirinita was utterly horrified.

Sensella sighed. "I should have known this would happen. I should never have let you hatch that egg in the first place. What *was* your father thinking of, bringing you a dragon's egg?"

"I don't know," Sirinita said. "Maybe he wasn't thinking anything."

Sensella chuckled sourly. "You're probably right, Siri. You're probably just exactly right." She glanced over at the dragon.

Tharn was trying to eat the curtains again.

Sirinita followed her mother's gaze. "Tharn!" she shouted. "Stop that this instant!"

The dragon stopped, startled, and turned to look at his mistress with his golden slit-pupilled eyes. The curtain, caught on one of his fangs, turned with him, and tore slightly. The dragon looked up at the curtain with an offended expression, and used a foreclaw to pry the fabric off his teeth.

Sensella sighed. Sirinita almost giggled, Tharn's expression was so funny, but then she remembered what was going to happen to her beloved dragon in a few days' time, and the urge to giggle vanished completely.

"Come on, Tharn," she said. "Let's go outside."

Sensella watched as her daughter and her pet ran out of the house onto the streets of Ethshar.

She hoped they wouldn't get into any trouble. Both of them meant well enough, but the dragon did have all those claws and teeth, and while it couldn't yet spit fire it was beginning to breathe hot vapor. And sometimes Sirinita just didn't think about the consequences of her actions.

But then, that was hardly a unique fault, or even one limited to children. Sensella wondered again just what Gar had thought he was doing when he brought back a dragon's egg from one of his trading expeditions.

One of the farmers had found it in the woods while berry-picking, Gar had said—had found a whole nest, in fact, though he wouldn't say what had happened to the other eggs. Probably sold them to wizards.

And why in the World had she and Gar let Sirinita *hatch* the egg, and keep the baby dragon long enough to become so attached? That had been very foolish indeed. Baby dragons were very fashionable, of course—parading through the streets with a dragon on a leash was the height of social display, and a sure way to garner invitations to all the right parties.

But the dowagers and matrons who did that didn't let their children make playmates of the little monsters! The sensible ones didn't use real dragons at all, they bought magical imitations, like that beautiful wood-and-lacquer thing Lady Nuvielle carried about, with its red glass eyes and splendid black wings. It moved and hissed and flew with a perfect semblance of life, thanks to a wizard's skill, and it didn't eat a thing, and would never grow an inch.

Tharn ate everything, grew constantly, and couldn't yet fly more than a few feet without tangling itself up in its own wings and falling out of the sky.

Sirinita adored it.

Sensella sighed again.

Outside, Sirinita and Tharn were racing down Wargate High Street, toward the Arena—and Tharn was almost winning, to Sirinita's surprise. He *was* getting bigger. He was at least as big as any dog Sirinita had ever seen—but then, she hadn't seen very many, and she had heard that out in the country dogs sometimes grew much larger than the ones inside the city walls.

Much as Sirinita hated to admit it, her mother was right. Tharn was getting too big to keep at home. He had knocked over the washbasin in her bedroom that morning, and Sirinita suspected that he'd eaten the neighbors' cat yesterday, though maybe the stuck-up thing was just hiding somewhere.

But did Tharn have to *die*, just because he was a dragon?

There had to be someplace a dragon could live.

She stopped, out of breath, at the corner of Center Street. Tharn tried to stop beside her, but tripped over his own fore-claws and fell in a tangle of wings and tail. Sirinita laughed, but a moment later Tharn was upright again, his head bumping scratchily against her hip. If she'd been wearing a lighter tunic, Sirinita thought, those sharp little scales would leave welts.

He really did have to go.

But where?

She peered down Center Street to the west; that led to the shipyards. Tharn would hardly be welcome there, especially if he started breathing fire around all that wood and pitch, but maybe somewhere out at sea? Was there some island where a dragon could live in safety, some other land where dragons were welcome?

Probably not.

There were stories about dragons that lived in the sea itself, but somehow she couldn't imagine Tharn being that sort. His egg had been found in a forest, after all, up near the Tintallionese border, and he'd never shown any interest in learning to swim.

The shipyards weren't any help.

In the other direction both Center Street and Wargate High Street led to the Arena—Wargate High Street led straight to the south side, four blocks away, while Center looped around and wound up on the north side after six blocks.

Could the Arena use a dragon?

That seemed promising. Dragons were impressive, and people liked to look at them.

At least, in pictures; in real life people tended to be too frightened of adult dragons to want to look at them.

But Tharn was a *tame* dragon, or at least Sirinita *hoped* he was tame. He wasn't dangerous, not really. Wouldn't he be a fine attraction in the Arena?

And she could come to visit him there, too!

That would be perfect.

"Come on, Tharn," she said, and together the girl and her dragon trotted on down Wargate High Street.

There wasn't a show today; the arena gates were closed, the tunnels and galleries deserted. Sirinita hadn't thought about that; she pressed up against a gate and stared through the iron at the shadowy passages beyond.

No one was in there.

She sat down on the hard-packed dirt of the street to think. Tharn curled up beside her, his head in her lap, the scales of his chin once again scratching her legs right through her tunic.

People turned to stare as they passed, then quickly looked away so as not to be rude. Sirinita was accustomed to this; after all, one didn't see a dragon on the streets of Ethshar every day, and certainly not one as big as Tharn was getting to be. She ignored them and sat thinking, trying to figure out who she should talk to about finding a place for Tharn at the Arena.

There was one fellow, however, who stopped a few feet away and asked, "Are you all right?"

Sirinita looked up, startled out of her reverie. "I'm fine, thank you," she said automatically.

The man who had addressed her was young, thin, almost handsome, and dressed in soft leather breeches and a tunic of brown velvet—a clean one, in good repair, so Sirinita could be reasonably certain that he wasn't poor, wasn't a beggar or any of the more dangerous inhabitants of the fields out beyond Wall Street.

Of course, people who lived in the fields rarely got this far in toward the center of the city. And there were plenty of dangerous people who didn't live in the fields.

She had Tharn to protect her, though, and she was only a few blocks from home.

"Is there anything I can help you with? You look worried," the man said.

"I'm fine," Sirinita repeated.

"Is it your dragon? Are you doing something magical?"

"He's my dragon, yes, but I was just thinking, not doing magic. I'm not even an apprentice yet, see?" She pointed to her bare legs—if she was too young for a woman's skirt, she was too young for an apprenticeship.

In fact, she was still a month short of her twelfth birthday and formal skirting, which was the very earliest she could possibly start an apprenticeship, and she hadn't yet decided if she wanted to learn *any* trade. She didn't think she wanted to learn magic, though; magic was dangerous.

"Oh," the man said, a bit sheepishly. "I thought…well, one doesn't see a lot of dragons, especially not that size. I thought maybe it was part of some spell."

Sirinita shook her head. "No. We were just thinking."

"About the Arena? There's to be a performance the day after tomorrow, I believe, in honor of Lord Wulran's birthday, but there's nothing today."

"I know," Sirinita said. "I mean, I'd forgotten, but I know now."

"Oh." The man looked at them uncertainly.

"Do you work in the Arena?" Sirinita asked, suddenly realizing this might be the opportunity she had been looking for.

"No, I'm afraid not. Did you want…." He didn't finish the sentence.

"We were wondering if Tharn could be in a show," Sirinita explained.

"Tharn?"

"My dragon."

"Ah." The man scratched thoughtfully at his beard. "Perhaps if you spoke to the Lord of the Games…"

"Who's he?"

“Oh, he’s the man in charge of the Arena,” the man explained. “Among other things. His name is Lord Varrin.”

“Do you know him?” Sirinita looked up hopefully.

“Well, yes,” the young man admitted.

“Could you introduce me?”

The young man hesitated, sighed, then said, “Oh, all right. Come on, then.”

Sirinita pushed Tharn’s head off her lap and jumped up eagerly.

Lord Varrin, it developed, lived just three blocks away, in a mansion at the corner of Wargate High Street and, of course, Games Street. A servant answered the door and bowed at the sight of the young man in velvet, then ushered man, girl, and dragon into the parlor.

A moment later Lord Varrin, a large, handsome man of middle years wearing black silk and leather, emerged and bowed.

“Lord Doran,” he said. “What brings you here?”

Sirinita’s head whirled about to look at the man in velvet. “Lord Doran?” she asked.

He nodded.

“The overlord’s brother?”

“I’m afraid so.”

“But I…um…”

“Never mind that,” Doran said gently. “Tell Lord Varrin why we’re here.”

“Oh.” Sirinita turned back to the Lord of the Games, grabbed Tharn by his head-crest to keep him from eating anything he shouldn’t, and explained.

When she had finished, Lords Varrin and Doran looked at one another.

“I’m afraid,” Lord Varrin said gently, “that your father is right; we don’t ever keep dragons inside the city walls. It simply isn’t safe. Even the most well-intentioned dragon can’t be trusted not to do some serious damage—quite by accident, usually. A full-grown dragon is *big*, young lady; just walking down a street its wings and tail could break windows and knock down signboards. And if it loses its temper—*anyone* can lose his temper sometimes."

Sirinita looked at Lord Doran for confirmation.

"There's nothing *I* can do," that worthy said. "I'm not even sure my brother could manage it, and I certainly can't. Our duty is to protect the city, and Lord Varrin is right—that means no large dragons. I'm very sorry."

"Not even for the Arena?" Sirinita asked.

Lord Varrin shook his head. "If we ever really needed a dragon," he said, "we could have one sent in from somewhere, just for the show. We wouldn't keep one here. And we'd have a dozen magicians standing guard every second, just in case."

"So Tharn has to die?"

Varrin and Doran looked at one another.

"Well," Doran said, "that's up to you and your father. We just know he can't stay inside the city walls once he's bigger than a grown man. That's the law."

"It's a *law*?"

"I'm afraid so."

"Oh." She looked down at her feet, dejected, then remembered her manners. "Thank you anyway," she said.

"You're welcome. I'm sorry we can't do more."

The servant escorted Sirinita and Tharn back out onto Wargate High Street, where she looked down at Tharn in despair and asked, "*Now* what?"

He snorted playfully, and the hot, fetid fumes made Sirinita cough. She also thought she might have seen an actual spark this time.

That would be the pebble that sank the barge, Sirinita thought—if her parents found out that Tharn was spitting sparks out his nose they wouldn't allow him in the house, and that "few days" her mother had mentioned would disappear. He'd be chopped up and sold to the wizards *today*, she was sure.

Ordinarily, when confronted with an insoluble problem, she might have thought about consulting a wizard herself. She couldn't afford their fees, but sometimes, if they weren't busy, they would talk to her anyway, and offer advice. She had never needed any actual magic, so she didn't know if they would have worked their wizardry for her.

This time, though, wizards were out of the question. They were the ones who wanted Tharn's blood for their spells. Lord Varrin had said that magicians could control dragons in the Arena, but if they could control them well enough to keep them in the city, wouldn't they have already done so?

Besides, there was that law—no grown dragons inside the city walls.

Well, then, Sirinita told herself, she would just have to get Tharn outside those walls!

She looked around.

Games Street led northeastward—didn't it go right to Eastgate? And of course, Wargate High Street went to Wargate, but Wargate was down in the guard camp with the soldiers; Sirinita didn't like to go there. She didn't mind the city guards most of the time, but when there were that many all in one place they made her nervous.

Eastgate should be all right, though. She had never been there, let alone out of the city, but it should be all right.

Grandgate or Newgate might be closer than Eastgate, but she didn't know the streets to find them. Eastgate was easy.

"Come on, Tharn," she said, and together they set out along Games Street.

It took the better part of an hour to reach Eastgate Plaza. Sirinita didn't think the distance was even a whole mile, but there were so many distractions!

Games Street, after all, was lined with gaming houses. There were cardrooms and dice halls and archery ranges and wrestling rings and any number of other entertainments, and there were people drifting in and out of them. One man who smelled of *oushka* offered to gamble with Sirinita, his gold against her dragon; she politely declined. And dragons weren't often seen in Eastside, so several people stopped to stare and ask her questions.

At last, however, she reached Eastgate Plaza, where a few farmers and tradesmen were peddling their wares in a dusty square beside the twin towers of Eastgate. It wasn't terribly busy; Sirinita supposed most of the business went on at the other squares and markets, such as Eastgate Circle, four blocks to the west, or Farmgate, or Market.

The gate towers were big forbidding structures of dark gray stone, either one of them several times the size of Sirinita's house, which wasn't small. The gates between them were bigger than any doors Sirinita had ever seen—and they were all standing open.

All she had to do was take Tharn out there, outside the walls, and he wouldn't have to be killed.

She marched forward resolutely, Tharn trotting at her heel.

Of course, it meant she would have to turn Tharn loose, and never see him again—*she* couldn't live outside the walls. Her mother would never allow it. Besides, there were pirates and monsters and stuff out there.

But at least he'd still be alive.

That was what she was thinking when she walked into the spear-shaft.

She blinked, startled, then started to duck under it, assuming that it was in her way by accident.

"Ho, there!" the guard who held the spear called, and he bent down and grabbed her arm with his other hand. "What's your hurry?"

"I need to get my dragon out of the city," Sirinita explained.

The guard looked at Tharn, then back at Sirinita. "Your dragon?"

"Yes. His name's Tharn. Let go of my arm." She tugged, but the guard's fingers didn't budge.

"Can't do that," he said. "Not yet, anyway. Part of my job is to keep track of any kids who enter or leave the city without their parents along. If, for example, you were to be running away from home, and your folks wanted to find you but couldn't afford to hire a magician to do it, it'd make things much easier on them if they could ask the guards at the gate, 'Did my girl come through here? A pretty thing in a blue tunic, about so tall?' And I'd be able to tell them, so they'd know whether you're inside or outside the city walls."

Sirinita blinked up at the man. He was a big, heavy fellow, with deep brown eyes and a somewhat ragged beard.

"What if I went out a different gate?" she asked.

"Oh, we report everything to the captain, and he tallies up the reports every day, so your folks could check the captain's list. Then they'd even know which gate you went out, which might give them an idea where you're going."

Sirinita said, "My name's Sirinita, and I'm just going out to find a place for my dragon. I'll be back by nightfall."

"Just Sirinita?"

"Sirinita of Ethshar. Except the neighbors call me Sirinita of the Dragon."

"I can understand that." The guard released her arm. "Go on, then."

Sirinita had gone no more than three steps when the man called after her, "Wait a minute."

"Now what is it?" she asked impatiently, turning back.

"What do you mean, 'find a place for your dragon'?"

"I mean find somewhere he can live. He can't stay in the city any more."

"You don't have any supplies."

Sirinita blinked up at him in surprise. "Supplies?"

"Right, supplies. It's a long way to anywhere it would be safe to turn a dragon loose."

"It is?" Sirinita was puzzled. "I was just going to take him outside the walls."

"What, on someone's farm, or in the middle of a village?"

"No, of course not," Sirinita said, but the guard's words were making her rethink the situation. She probably *would* have just turned Tharn loose on someone's farm.

But that wouldn't be a good idea, would it?

"Um," she said. "I'm going to take him to my grandfather, I'm not going to turn him loose."

Her grandfathers both lived in the city—one was a Seagate merchant, the other owned a large and successful carpentry business in Crafton—but she didn't see any reason to tell the guard that.

"Your grandfather's got a farm near here?"

Sirinita nodded.

The guard considered her for a moment, then turned up an empty palm. "All right," he said. "Go ahead, then."

"Thank you." She turned eastward once again, and marched out of the city.

She wondered what sort of supplies the guard had meant. Whatever they were, she would just have to do without them. It couldn't be *that* far to somewhere she could turn Tharn loose.

She looked out across the countryside, expecting to see a few farms and villages—she had seen pictures, and had a good idea what they should look like, with their half-timbered houses and pretty green fields.

What she actually saw, however, was something else entirely.

The road out of the city was a broad expanse of bare, hard-packed dirt crossed here and there with deep, muddy ruts. A few crude houses built of scrap wood were scattered around, and people stood or crouched in doorways, hawking goods and services to passersby—goods and services that were not allowed in the city, and Ethshar was a fairly tolerant place.

A hundred yards from the city the farms began—not with quaint cottages and tidy little fields, but with endless rows of stubby green plants in black dirt, and rough wooden sheds set here and there. The only roads were paths just wide enough for a wagon.

Sirinita was surprised, but walked on, Tharn at her heels.

She was still walking, hours later, when the sun sank below the hills she had already crossed. She was dirty and exhausted and miserable.

She had finally reached farms that more or less resembled those in the pictures, at any rate—not so clean or so charming, but at least there were thatched farmhouses and barns, and the fields no longer stretched unbroken to the horizon.

But she hadn't reached forests or mountains or even a fair-sized grove. The only trees were windbreaks or orchards or shade trees around houses. As far as she could see, from any hilltop she checked, there were only more farms—except to the west, of course, where she could sometimes, from the higher hills, still see the city walls, and where she thought she could occasionally catch the gleam of sunlight on the sea.

And everything smelled of the cow manure the farmers used as fertilizer.

The World, she thought bitterly, was obviously bigger than she had realized. No wonder her father's trading expeditions lasted a month at a time!

Tharn had not enjoyed taking so long a walk, either; he was a healthy and active young dragon, but he was still accustomed to taking an afternoon nap, to resting when he felt like it. He had not appreciated it when his mistress had dragged him along, and had even kicked him when he tried to sleep.

When the sun went down, he had had enough; he flopped onto a hillock, mashing some farmer's pumpkin vines, and curled up to sleep.

Sirinita, too exhausted for anger or protest, looked down at him and started crying.

Tharn paid no attention. He slept.

When she was done weeping, Sirinita sat down beside her dragon and looked about in the gathering gloom.

She couldn't see anyone, anywhere. They weren't on a road any more, just a path through somebody's fields, and she couldn't see anything but half-grown crops and the shadowy shapes of distant farmhouses. Some of the windows were lighted, others dark, but nowhere did she see a torch or signboard over a door—if any of these places were inns, or even just willing to admit weary travelers, she didn't know how to tell.

She was out here in the middle of nowhere, miles from her soft clean bed, miles from her parents, her friends, *everybody*, with just her stupid dragon to keep her company, and it was all because he was growing too fast.

Tharn wouldn't even stay awake so she could talk to him. She kicked him, purely out of spite; he puffed in annoyance, emitting a few sparks, but didn't wake.

That was new; he hadn't managed actual sparks before, so far as she could remember.

It didn't matter, though. She wasn't going any further with him. In the morning she was going to turn him loose, just leave him here and go home, maybe even slip away while he was asleep. If the farmers didn't like having him around, maybe they'd chase him off to the wilderness, wherever it was.

And maybe they'd kill him, but at least he'd have a *chance*, and she just couldn't go any farther.

Tharn breathed out another tiny shower of sparks, and a stench of something foul reached Sirinita's nostrils; Tharn's breath, never pleasant to begin with, was getting really disgusting—

even worse than the cow manure, which she had mostly gotten used to.

Sirinita decided there wasn't any need to sleep right next to the dragon; she wandered a few paces away, to where a field of waist-high cornstalks provided some shelter, and settled down for the night.

The next thing she knew was that an unfamiliar voice was saying, "I don't see a lantern."

She opened a sleepy eye, and saw nothing at all.

"So maybe she just burned a cornstalk or something," a second voice said.

"I don't even see a tinderbox," the first replied.

"I don't either, but what do I know? I saw sparks here, and here she is—it must've been her. Maybe she had some little magic spell or something—she looks like a city girl."

"Maybe there was someone with her."

"No, she wouldn't be lying here all alone, then. No one would be stupid enough to leave a girl unprotected."

The first voice giggled unpleasantly. "Not if they knew *we* were around, certainly."

"She's pretty young," the second said dubiously.

Sirinita was completely awake now; she realized she was looking at the rich black earth of the farm. She turned her head, very carefully, to see who was speaking.

"She's awake!" the first voice said. "Quick!"

Then rough hands grabbed her, and her tunic was yanked up, trapping her arms, covering her face so that she couldn't see, and pulling her halfway to her feet. Unseen hands clamped around her wrists, holding the tunic up.

"Not all *that* young," someone said, but Sirinita couldn't hear well enough through the tunic to be sure which voice it was. Another hand touched her now-bare hip.

Sirinita screamed.

Someone hit her on the back of the head hard enough to daze her.

Then she heard Tharn growl.

It wasn't a sound she had heard often; it took a lot to provoke the dragon, as a rule.

"What was that?" one of her attackers asked.

"It's a baby dragon," the other replied. The grip on her left wrist fell away, and she was able to pull her tunic partway down, below her eyes.

She was in the cornfield, and it was still full night, but the greater moon shone orange overhead, giving enough light to make out shapes, but not colors.

There were two men, *big* men, and they both had swords, and Tharn was facing them, growling, his tail lashing snakelike behind him. One of the men was holding her right wrist with his left hand, drawing his sword with his right.

The other man, sword already drawn, was approaching Tharn cautiously.

"Dragon's blood," he said. "The wizards pay good money for dragon's blood."

He stepped closer, closer—and Tharn's curved neck suddenly straightened, thrusting his scaly snout to a foot or so from the man's face, and Tharn spat flame, lighting up the night, momentarily blinding the three humans, whose eyes had all been adjusted to the darkness.

The man who had approached the dragon screamed horribly, and the other dropped Sirinita's wrist; thus abruptly released, she stumbled and almost fell.

When she was upright and able to see again, she saw one man kneeling, both hands covering his face as he continued to scream; his sword was nowhere in sight. The other man was circling, trying to get behind Tharn, or at least out of the line of fire.

Tharn was growling differently now, a sound like nothing Sirinita had ever heard before. His jaws and nostrils were glowing dull red, black smoke curled up from them, and his eyes caught the moonlight and gleamed golden. He didn't look like her familiar, bumbling pet; he looked terrifying.

The uninjured man dove for Tharn's neck, and the dragon turned with incredible speed, belching flame.

The man's hair caught fire, but he dived under the gout of flame and stabbed at Tharn.

Tharn dodged, or tried to, but Sirinita heard the metal blade scrape sickeningly across those armored scales she had so often scratched herself on.

Then Tharn, neck fully extended and bent almost into a circle, took his attacker from behind and closed his jaws on the man's neck.

Sirinita screamed—she didn't know why, she just did.

The first man was still whimpering into his hands.

The second man didn't scream, though; he just made a soft grunting noise, then sagged lifelessly across Tharn's back. His hair was smoldering; a shower of red sparks danced down Tharn's flank.

Sirinita turned and ran.

At first she wasn't running anywhere in particular; then she spotted a farmhouse with a light in the window. Someone had probably been awakened by the screaming. She turned her steps toward it.

A moment later she was hammering her fists on the door.

"Who is it?" someone called. "I've got a sword and a spear here."

"Help!" Sirinita shrieked.

For a moment no one answered, but she heard muffled voices debating; then the door burst open and she fell inside.

"They attacked me," she said. "And Tharn killed one of them, and...and..."

"Who attacked you?" a woman asked.

"Two men. Big men."

"Who's Tharn? Your father?" a man asked.

"My pet dragon."

The man and the woman looked at one another.

"She's crazy," the man said.

"Close the door," the woman answered.

"You don't think I should try to help?"

"Do you hear anyone else screaming?"

The man listened; so did Sirinita.

"No," the man said. "But I hear noises."

"Let them take care of it themselves, then."

"But...." The man hesitated, then asked, "Was anyone hurt?"

"The men who attacked me. Tharn hurt them both. I think he killed one."

"But this Tharn was all right when you left?" the woman asked.

Sirinita nodded.

"Then leave well enough alone for now. We'll go out in the morning and see what's what. Or if this Tharn comes to the door and speaks fair—we've the girl to tell us if it's the right one."

The man took one reluctant final look out the door, then closed and barred it, while the woman soothed Sirinita and led her to a corner by the fire where she could lie down. The man found two blankets and a feather pillow, and Sirinita curled up, shivering, certain she would never sleep again.

She was startled to wake up to broad daylight.

"You told us the truth last night," her hostess remarked.

Sirinita blinked sleep from her eyes.

"About your dragon, I mean. He's curled up out front. At first my man was afraid to step past him, after what you'd said about his fighting those two men, but he looks harmless enough, so at last he ventured it."

"I'm sorry he troubled you," Sirinita said.

"No trouble," she said.

"I have to get home," Sirinita said, as she sat up.

"No hurry, is there?"

Sirinita hesitated. "It's a long walk back to the city."

"It is," the woman admitted. "But isn't that all the more reason to have breakfast first?"

Sirinita, who had had no supper the night before, did not argue with that; she ate a hearty meal of hot buttered cornbread, apples, and cider.

When she was done she tried to feed Tharn, but the dragon wasn't hungry.

When the farmer showed her what he had found in the cornfield she saw why. Both her attackers were sprawled there—or at any rate, what was left of them. Tharn was still a very small dragon; he had left quite a bit.

She looked down at the dragon at her side; Tharn looked up at her and blinked. He stretched his wings and belched a small puff of flame.

"Come on," Sirinita said. She waved a farewell to her hosts—she never had learned their names, though she thought they'd been mentioned—then started walking up her own shadow, heading westward toward Ethshar.

It was late afternoon when, footsore and frazzled, she reached Eastgate with Tharn still at her heel. She made her way down East Road to the city's heart, then turned south into the residential district that had always been her home.

Her parents were waiting.

"When you weren't home by midnight we were worried, so this morning we hired a witch," her mother explained, after embraces and greetings had been exchanged. "She said you'd be home safe some time today, and here you are." She looked past her daughter at the dragon. "And Tharn, too, I see." She hesitated, then continued, "The witch said that Tharn saved your life last night. We really *can't* keep him here, Siri, but we can find a home for him somewhere...."

"No," Sirinita interrupted, hugging her mother close. "No, don't do that." She closed her eyes, and images of the man with the burned face screaming, the other man with his hair on fire and his neck broken, the two of them lying half-eaten between the rows of corn, appeared.

Tharn had been protecting her, and those men had meant to rape her and maybe kill her, but she knew those images would always be there.

Tharn was a dragon, and that was what dragons did.

"No, Mother," she said, shuddering, tears leaking from the corners of her eyes. "Get a wizard and have him killed."

About "Portrait of a Hero"

Lester del Rey, my editor at the time, had discovered an artist whose work he really liked, by the name of Michael Pangrazio. He wanted to do a project to showcase the guy's work, so he got together with his assistant Risa Kessler (at least, I think she was his assistant; I never dealt with her directly) and put together an anthology called Once Upon A Time*, which would feature "modern fairy tales" by all Del Rey's top fantasy authors. Each story would be illustrated with a painting by Michael Pangrazio. I was very flattered to be included in this, but wasn't sure about writing a "modern fairy tale." On the other hand, one of my sisters had asked me to write a story with a prophecy in it, so I had started one that I had originally intended to be a novel, but once I started working on it I realized it didn't have enough plot for a novel. I abandoned it unfinished.*

When Once Upon A Time *came along I finished the prophecy story, cut it down even more, and sent it to Lester, who bought it. My sister got her prophecy novel a few years later, in the form of* Taking Flight.

PORTRAIT OF A HERO

1.

The dragon atop the mountain loomed over the village like a tombstone over a grave, and Wuller looked up at it in awe.

"Do you think it'll come any closer?" he whispered to his aunt.

Illuré shook her head.

"There's no telling, with dragons," she said. "Particularly not the really big ones. One that size must be as experienced and cunning as any human that ever lived."

Something was odd about her voice. Wuller glanced at her face, which was set in a rigid calm, and realized that his aunt Illuré, who had faced down a runaway boar with nothing but a turnspit, was terrified.

Even as he looked, her calm broke; her eyes went wide, her mouth started to open.

Wuller whirled back in time to see the dragon rising from its perch, its immense wings spread wide to catch the wind. It rose, wheeled about once, and then swept down toward the village, claws outstretched, like a hawk diving on its prey.

For a moment Wuller thought it was diving directly at *him*, and he covered his face with his hands, as if he were still a child.

Then he remembered how high that mountaintop was, and his mind adjusted the scale of what he had just seen—the dragon was larger and farther than he had assumed. Ashamed of his terror, he dropped his hands and looked up again.

The dragon was hovering over the village, directly over his own head. Wuller felt a tugging at one arm, and realized that Illuré was trying to pull him out from under the great beast.

He yielded, and a moment later the creature settled to the ground in the village common, the wind from its wings stirring up a cloud of grey dust and flattening the thin grass. The scent of its hot, sulphurous breath filled the town.

A swirl of dust reached Wuller, and he sneezed.

The dragon's long neck dipped down, and its monstrous head swung around to look Wuller directly in the eye from a mere six or seven feet away.

He stared back, frozen with fear.

Then the head swung away again, the neck lifted it up, and the mighty jaws opened.

The dragon spoke.

"Who speaks for this village?" it said, in a voice like an avalanche.

"It talks!" someone said, in tones of awe and wonder.

The dragon's head swept down to confront the speaker, and it spoke again.

"Yes, I talk," it rumbled. "Do you?"

Wuller looked to see who it was addressing, and saw a young man in blue—his cousin Pergren, just a few years older than himself, who had only recently started his own flock.

Pergren stammered, unable to answer coherently, and the dragon's jaws crept nearer and nearer to him. Wuller saw that they were beginning to open—not to speak, this time, but to bite.

Then a man stepped forward—Adar, the village smith, Wuller's father's cousin.

"I'll speak for the village, dragon," he called. "Leave that boy alone and say what you want of us."

Wuller had always admired Adar's strength and skill; now he found himself admiring the smith's courage, as well.

The dragon reared up slightly, and Wuller thought it looked slightly amused. "Well!" it said. "One among you with manners enough to speak when spoken to—though hardly in a civil tone!"

"Get on with it," Adar said.

"All right, if you're as impatient as all that," the dragon said. "I had intended to make a few polite introductions before getting down to business, but have it your way. I have chosen this village as my home. I have chosen you people as my servants. And I have come down here today to set the terms of your service. Is that clear and direct enough to suit you, man?"

Wuller tried to judge the dragon's tone, to judge whether it was speaking sarcastically, but the voice was simply too different from human for him to tell.

"We are not servants," Adar announced. "We are free people."

"Not any more," the dragon said.

2.

Wuller shuddered again at the memory of Adar's death, then turned his attention back to the meeting that huddled about the single lantern in his father's house.

"We can't go on like this," his father was saying. "At a sheep a day, even allowing for a better lambing season next spring than the one we just had, we'll have nothing left at all after three years, not even a breeding pair to start anew!"

"What would you have us do, then?" old Kirna snapped at him. "You heard what it said after it ate Adar. One sheep a day, or one person, and it doesn't care which!"

"We need to kill it," Wuller's father said.

"Go right ahead, Wulran," someone called from the darkness. "We won't mind a bit if you kill it!"

"I can't kill it, any more than you can," Wuller's father retorted, "but surely *someone* must be able to! Centuries ago, during the war, dragons were used in battle by both sides, and both sides killed great numbers of them. It can be done, and I'm sure the knowledge isn't lost…"

"*I'm* not sure of that!" Kirna interrupted.

"All right, then," Wulran shouted, "maybe it *is* lost! But look at us here! The whole lot of us packed together in the dark because we don't dare light a proper council fire, for fear of that beast! Our livestock are taken one by one, day after day, and when the sheep run out it will start on *us*—it's said as much! Already we're left with no smith but a half-trained apprentice boy, because of that thing that lurks on the mountain. We're dying slowly, the whole lot of us—would it be that much worse to risk dying quickly?"

An embarrassed silence was the only reply.

"All right, Wulran," someone muttered at last, "what do you want us to *do*?"

Wuller looked at his father expectantly, and was disappointed to see the slumped shoulders and hear the admission, "I don't know."

"Maybe if we *all* attacked it…" Wuller suggested.

"Attacked it with *what*?" Pergren demanded. "Our bare hands?"

Wuller almost shouted back, "Yes," but he caught himself at the last moment and stayed silent.

"Is there any magic we could use?" little Salla, who was barely old enough to attend the meeting, asked hesitantly. "In the stories, the heroes who go to fight dragons always have magic swords, or enchanted armor."

"We have no magic swords," Illuré said.

"Wait a minute," Alasha the Fair said. "We don't have a sword, but we have magic, of a sort." Wuller could not be certain in the darkness, but thought she was looking at her sister Kirna as she spoke.

"Oh, now, wait a minute…" Kirna began.

"What's she talking about, Kirna?" Pergren demanded.

"Kirna?" Illuré asked, puzzled.

Kirna glanced at the faces that were visible in the lantern's glow, and at the dozens beyond, and gave in.

"All right," she said, "but it won't do any good. I'm not even sure it still works."

"Not sure *what* still works?" someone asked.

"The oracle," Kirna replied.

"*What* oracle?" someone demanded, exasperated.

"I'll show you," she answered, rising. "It's at my house; I'll go fetch it."

"No," Wulran said, with authority, "we'll come with you. All of us. We'll move the meeting there."

Kirna started to protest, then glanced about and thought better of it.

"All right," she said.

3.

The thing gleamed in the lantern-light, and Wuller stared, fascinated. He had never seen anything magical before.

The oracle was a block of polished white stone—or polished *something*, anyway; it wasn't any stone that Wuller was familiar with. A shallow dish of the smoothest, finest glass he had ever seen was set into the top of the stone, glass with only a faint tinge of green to it and without a single bubble or flaw.

Kirna handled it with extreme delicacy, holding it only by the sides of the block and placing it gently onto the waiting pile of furs.

"It's been in my family since the Great War," she said quietly. "One of my ancestors took it from the tent of a northern sorcerer when the Northern Empire fell and the victorious Ethsharites swept through these lands, driving the enemy before them."

"What is it?" someone whispered.

"It's an oracle," Kirna said. "A sorcerer's oracle."

"Do we need a sorcerer to work it, then?"

"No," Kirna said, staring at the glass dish and gently brushing her fingers down one side of the block. "My mother taught me how."

She stopped and looked up.

"And it's very old, and very delicate, and very precious, and we don't know how many more questions it can answer, if it can still answer any at all, so don't get your hopes up! We've been saving it for more than a hundred years!"

"Keeping it for yourselves, you mean!"

"And why not?" Alasha demanded, coming to her sister's defense. "It was our family's legacy, not the village's! We've brought it out now, when it's needed, haven't we?"

Nobody argued with that.

"Go on, Kirna," Wulran said quietly. "Ask it."

"Ask it what, exactly?" she replied.

"Ask it who will save us from the dragon," Pergren said. "None of us know how to kill it; ask it who can rid us of it."

Kirna looked around and saw several people nod. "All right," she said. She turned to the oracle, placed her hands firmly on either side of the block, and stared intently down into the glass dish.

Wuller was close enough to look over her left shoulder, while Illuré looked over her right, and Alasha and Wulran faced them on the other side of the oracle. All five watched the gleaming disk, while the rest of the crowd stood back, clearly more than a little nervous before this strange device. Wuller's mother Mereth, in particular, was pressed back against the wall of the room, busily fiddling with the fancywork on her blouse to work off her nervousness.

"*Pau'ron*," Kirna said. "*Yz'raksis nyuyz'r, lai brinan allasis!*"

The glass dish suddenly began to glow with a pale, eerie light. Wuller heard someone gasp.

"It's ready," Kirna said, looking up.

"Ask it," Wulran told her.

Kirna looked about, shifted her knees to a more comfortable position, then stared into the dish again.

"We are beset by a dragon," she said loudly. "Who can rid us of it?"

Wuller held his breath and stared as faint bluish shapes appeared in the dish, shifting shapes like clouds on a windy day, or the smoke from a blown-out candle. Some of them seemed to form runes, but these broke apart before he could read them.

"I can't make it out," Kirna shouted. "Show us more clearly!"

The shapes suddenly coalesced into a single image, a pale oval set with two eyes and a mouth. Details emerged, until a face looked up out of the dish at them, the face of a young woman, not much older than Wuller himself, a delicate face surrounded by billows of soft brown hair. Her eyes were a rich green, as green as the moss that grew on the mountainside.

Wuller thought he had never seen anyone so beautiful.

Then the image vanished, the glow vanished, and the glass dish shattered into a dozen jagged fragments.

Kirna let out a long wail of grief at the oracle's destruction, while Illuré called, "Find me paper! I must draw the face before we forget it!"

4.

Wuller stared at the portrait. Illuré had come very close, he thought, but she had not quite captured the true beauty of the face he had seen in the glass.

"Who is she?" Pergren asked. "It's no one in the village, certainly, nor anyone I ever saw before."

"Whoever she is, how can *she* possibly kill a hundred-foot dragon?" Pergren's brother Gennar demanded.

"Maybe she's a magician," Pergren suggested.

"There must be more powerful magicians in the World than her, though," Gennar objected. "If it just takes magic, why didn't the oracle say so? Why not show us some famous powerful wizard?"

"Maybe she *won't* kill it," Alasha said. "Kirna asked who could *rid* us of the dragon, not who could *slay* it."

Gennar snorted. "You think she'll *talk* it into going away?"

"Maybe," Alasha said. "Or maybe there's another way."

Pergren and Gennar turned to stare at her. Wuller was still looking at the picture.

Illuré certainly had a talent for drawing, he thought; the charcoal really looked like shadows and soft hair.

"What do you mean?" Pergren asked Alasha.

"I mean, that in some of the old stories, there are tales of sacrifices to dragons, where when a beautiful virgin willingly gave herself to the monster the beast was overcome by her purity, and either died or fled after devouring her."

Pergren glanced at the picture. "You think that's what she's to do, then? Sacrifice herself to the dragon?"

Gennar snorted. "That's silly," he said.

"No, it's magic," Alasha retorted.

"Why don't you sacrifice *yourself*, then, if you think it'll work?" Gennar demanded.

"I said a *virgin*," Alasha pointed out.

"She said beautiful, too," Pergren said, grinning. Alasha tossed a pebble at him.

"We have a couple of virgins here," Gennar said. "At least, I *think* we do."

"Virgins or not," Pergren said, "the oracle said that *she* would rid us of the dragon." He pointed to the picture Wuller held.

"No," said Alasha, "it said she *could* rid us of the dragon, not *would*."

That sobered all of them.

"So how do we find her?" Pergren asked. "Do we just sit here and wait for her to walk into the village, while that monster eats a sheep a day?"

"I'll go look for her," Wuller said.

The other three turned to him, startled.

"You?" Gennar asked.

"Why not?" Wuller replied. "I'm small enough to slip away without the dragon noticing me, and I'm not doing anything important around here anyway."

"How do you expect to find her, though?" Pergren asked. "It's a big world out there."

Wuller shrugged. "I don't know, for sure," he admitted, "but if we had that oracle here, then surely there will be ways to find her in the cities of the south."

Gennar squinted at him. "Are you sure you aren't just planning to slip away and forget all about us, once you're safely away?"

Wuller didn't bother to answer that; he just swung for Gennar's nose.

Gennar ducked aside, and Wuller's fist grazed his cheek harmlessly.

"All right, all right!" Gennar said, raising his hands, "I apologize!"

Wuller glared at him for a moment, then turned back to the portrait.

"I think Wuller's right," Pergren said. "*Somebody* has to go find her, and I've heard enough tales about the wizards of Ethshar to think that he's right, finding a magician is the way to do it."

"Why him, though?" Gennar demanded.

"Because he volunteered first," Pergren said. "Besides, he's right, he *is* small and sneaky. Remember when he stole your laces, and hid in that bush, and you walked right past him, looking for him, half a dozen times?"

Gennar conceded the point with a wave of his hand.

"It's not up to us, though," he said. "It's up to the elders. You think old Wulran's going to let his only son go off by himself?"

Alasha whispered, looking at Wuller, "He just might."

5.

In fact, Wulran was not enthusiastic about the idea when it was brought up at the meeting that night, and started to object.

His wife leaned over and whispered in his ear, cutting him off short.

He stopped, startled, and listened to her; then he looked at Wuller's face and read the solid determination there.

He shut his mouth and sat, silent and unhappy, as the others thrashed the matter out, and the next morning he embraced Wuller, then watched as the boy vanished among the trees.

It was really much easier than Wuller had expected; the dragon never gave any sign of noticing his departure at all. He just walked away, not even hiding—though he did stay under the trees, hidden from the sky.

At first, he simply walked, marking a tree-branch with his knife every few yards and heading southwest—south, because that was where all the cities were, and west to get down out of the mountains. He didn't worry about a particular destination, or what he was going to do for food, water, or shelter. He knew that the supplies he carried with him would only last for two or three days, and that it would probably take much longer than that to find a magician, but he just couldn't bring himself to think about that in his excitement over actually leaving the village and the dragon behind.

He took the charcoal sketch out of his pack, unrolled it, and studied it as he ambled onward beneath the pines.

Whoever the girl was, she was certainly beautiful, he thought. He wondered how long it would take him to find her.

He never doubted that he would find her eventually; after all, he had the portrait, and magic was said to be capable of almost anything. If one ancient sorcerous device could provide her image, surely modern wizardry, or some other sort of magic, would be able to locate her!

An hour or so from home he stopped for a rest, sitting down on the thick carpet of pine needles between two big roots and leaning back against the trunk of the tree he had just marked.

He had worked up an appetite already, but he resisted the temptation to eat anything. He hadn't brought that much food, and would need to conserve it.

Of course, he would get some of his food from the countryside, or at least that was what he had planned. Perhaps he could find something right here where he sat.

Glancing around he saw a small patch of mushrooms, and he leaned over for a closer look—he knew most of the local varieties, and some of them were quite tasty, even raw.

This variety he recognized immediately, and he shuddered and didn't touch them. They might be tasty, but nobody had ever lived long enough to say after eating them. Illuré had told him that this particular sort, with the thin white stem and the little cup at the bottom, held the most powerful poison known to humanity.

He decided he wasn't quite so hungry after all, and instead he took a drink from his water flask; surely, finding drinking water would be easy enough! If he kept on heading downhill, sooner or later he would find a stream.

Far more important than food or water, he thought, was deciding where to go. He had talked about going all the way to Ethshar, but that was hundreds of miles away; no one from the village had *ever* been to Ethshar. Surely he wouldn't really need to go that far!

He looked about, considering.

His home, he knew, was in the region of Srigmor, which had once been claimed by the Baronies of Sardiron. The claim had been abandoned long ago; the North Mines weren't worth the trouble of working, when the mines of Tazmor and Aldagmor were so much richer and more accessible, and Srigmor had nothing else that a baron would consider worth the trouble of surviving a winter there.

Sardiron was still there to the south, though.

To the west lay unnamed, uninhabited forests; he did not want to go there. True, beyond them lay the seacoast, and there might be people there, but it would be a long, hard, dangerous journey, and he knew nothing about what he might find there.

To the southwest the forests were said to end after about three days' travel, opening out onto the plain of Aala. If Srigmor were part of any nation now, it was part of Aala.

He had never heard of any magicians living in Aala, though. He tended to associate magicians with cities and castles, not with farms and villages, and Aala had no cities or castles.

The Baronies of Sardiron it would be, then.

His grandfather had visited Sardiron once, had made the long trip to the Council City itself, Sardiron of the Waters. If his grandfather could do it, so could he.

He stood up, brushed off pine needles, and marched onward, now heading almost directly south.

6.

Streams were harder to find than he had thought, and not all were as clean as he liked; after the first day he made it a point to fill his flask at every opportunity, and to drink enough at each clear stream to leave himself feeling uncomfortably bloated.

His food ran out at breakfast the third day, and he discovered edible mushrooms weren't as common as he had expected—though the poisonous ones seemed plentiful enough—and that rabbits and squirrels and chipmunks were harder to catch than he had realized. Skinning and cooking them was also far more work than he had expected it to be; the hunters and cooks at home had made it look so easy!

He almost broke his belt knife when it slipped while he was holding a dead squirrel on a large rock as he tried to gut it; he felt the shock in his wrist as the blade slipped and then snagged hard on a seam in the rock, and he held his breath, afraid that he had snapped off the tip.

He hadn't, but from then on he was more careful. The knife was an absolutely essential item now. He wished he had had the sense to borrow another, so as to have a spare.

He had made good time the first two days, but after that much of his effort went to hunting, cooking, eating, and finding someplace safe to sleep. He dropped from seven or eight leagues a day to about four.

He had expected to find villages, where he could ask for food and shelter. He didn't. He knew that there were villages within three or four leagues of his own, and assumed there were more scattered all through Srigmor, but somehow he never managed to come across any. He saw distant smoke several times, but never managed to find its source.

By the third night he was very tired indeed of sleeping on dead leaves or pine needles, wrapped in his one thin blanket. Even in the mild weather of late spring, the nights could be chilly—so chilly that only utter exhaustion let him sleep.

Late on the afternoon of the fourth day, though, his luck finally changed. He saw a break in the forest cover ahead and turned toward it, since such openings were often made by fallen trees that rotted out and became home to various edible creatures.

This opening, however, was not made by just *one* fallen tree. Rather, an entire line had been cleared away, and the surface below was completely free of debris. It was a long ribbon of hard-packed dirt edged by grass, with two shallow ruts running parallel for its entire length, and Wuller realized with a start that he was looking at a highway.

His spirits soared; checking his bearings from the sun, he set out southward on the road, certain that he would find other people to talk to within minutes. In his eager confidence, he did not worry about finding supper.

The minutes passed, and added up into hours, as the sun vanished below the trees to his right, while he encountered no one at all.

At last, long after dark, he gave up. He found himself a clear spot by the roadside where he unpacked his blanket and curled up in it, still hungry.

Despite his hunger, he slept.

7.

He was awakened by laughter. He sat up, startled and groggy, and looked about.

An ox-drawn wagon was passing him by. A man and a woman sat on its front bench, leaning against each other as the woman giggled.

"I like that, Okko!" she said. "Know any more?"

"Sure," the man replied. "Ever hear the one about the witch, the wainwright, and the Tazmorite? It seems that the three of them were on a raft floating down the river when the raft started to sink..."

Wuller shook his head to get the bits of grass and leaves out of his hair, stood up, and called out, "*Hai*! Over here!"

The man stopped his story and turned to see who had called, but did not stop his pair of oxen. The woman bent quickly down behind the bench, as if looking for something.

"Wait a minute!" Wuller called.

The man snorted. "Not likely!" he said. The wagon trundled on, heading north.

With a quick glance at his unpacked belongings and another down the highway to the south, Wuller ran after the wagon, easily catching up to it.

The driver still refused to stop, and the woman had sat up again, holding a cocked crossbow across her lap.

"Look," Wuller said as he walked alongside, "I'm lost and hungry and I need help. My village is being held hostage by a dragon, and I…"

"Don't tell me your troubles, boy," the driver said. "I've got my own problems."

"But couldn't you help me? I need to find a magician, so I can find this girl…" He realized he had left the sketch with his pack, back where he had slept. "If you could give me a ride to Sardiron…"

The driver snorted again. "Sardiron! Boy, take a look which way we're going! We're heading for Srigmor to trade with the natives, we aren't going back to Sardiron. And I'm no magician, and I don't know anything about any magicians. We can't help you, boy; sorry."

"But I just came down from Srigmor, and I don't know my way…"

The driver turned and stared at Wuller for a moment. The oxen plodded on.

"You just came from Srigmor?" he asked.

"Yes, I did, and…"

"There's a dragon there? Where? Which village?"

A sudden rush of hope made Wuller's feet light as he paced alongside. "It doesn't really have a name—it's not on the highway…"

"Oh!" the man said, clearly relieved. "One of the back country villages, up in the hills?"

"I guess so," Wuller admitted.

"Then it won't bother *me*," the driver said. "Sorry, it's not my problem. You go on south and find your magician." He turned his eyes back to the road, and said to the woman, "As I was saying, the raft starts to sink, and they're too far from shore to swim. So the witch goes into a trance and works a spell to keep it afloat, and the wainwright gets out his tools and starts trying to patch the leaks and caulk it all up, but the Tazmorite just sits there…"

Wuller stopped, and watched in dismay as the wagon rolled on northward.

He had not expected a reaction like that.

On the rare occasions when an outsider happened into his native village, he or she was invariably made to feel welcome, given the best food, drink, and shelter that the village could offer. He had expected to receive the same treatment in the outside world.

It appeared that he had misjudged.

Or perhaps, he told himself, that rather hostile pair was a fluke, an aberration. Surely, most people would be more generous!

He turned and headed back down the road, collected his belongings, and marched on southward toward Sardiron, certain that the pair in the wagon could not be typical.

8.

The pair in the wagon had not been typical; most people either wouldn't talk to him at all, or shouted at him to go away.

It didn't help any that all the traffic he encountered was northbound.

By mid-afternoon he had met half a dozen such rejections, and gone a full day without food. He was debating with himself whether he should leave the road to hunt something when he glimpsed a building ahead, standing at the roadside.

He quickened his pace a little.

A moment later he spotted a second building, and a third—an entire village!

Fifteen minutes later he stood on the cobblestones of the village square, looking about in fascination.

Roads led off to north, south, and east; he had come in from the north, and to the south lay Sardiron of the Waters, but where did the eastern road go? The mountains lay to the east, and while they did not look as tall here as they did back home, surely that was just a matter of distance. Why would anyone want to go into the mountains?

The square itself amazed him. He had never seen cobblestones before; the only pavement back home was the slate floor of the smithy. Here, a broad circle, perhaps a hundred feet across, was completely cobbled. He marvelled at the work that must have gone into the job.

At the center of the circle was a fountain, and he marvelled at that, too. He wondered how they made the water spray up like that; was it magic? If it was magic, would it be safe to drink?

Houses and shops surrounded the square, and those, while less marvelous, were strange; they were built of wood, of course, but the end of each beam was carved into fantastic shapes, like flowers or ferns or faces. He recognized the smithy readily enough by its open walls and glowing forge, and the bakery was distinguished by the enticing aroma and the broad window display of breads and cakes, but some of the other shops puzzled him. The largest of all, adjoining a shed or barn of some sort, bore a signboard with no runes on it at all, but simply a picture of a lone pine tree surrounded by flames.

Curious, he took a few steps toward this peculiar establishment.

An unfamiliar animal thrust its head over the top of a pen in the adjoining shed, and suddenly something clicked into place in Wuller's mind.

That was a horse, he realized. The shed was a stable. And the building, surely, must be an inn!

He had never seen a horse, a stable, or an inn before, but he had no doubt of his guess. An inn would give him food and a place to sleep; he marched directly toward the door.

The proprietor of the Burning Pine blinked at the sight of the peasant lad. The boy looked perhaps fifteen, and most northern peasants kept their sons at home until they were eighteen; if one was out on the road at a younger age it usually meant a runaway or an orphan.

Neither runaways nor orphans had much money, as a rule. "What do *you* want?" the innkeeper demanded.

Startled, Wuller turned and saw a plump old man in an apron. "Ah...dinner, to start with," he said.

"You have the money to pay for it?"

Wuller had never used money in his life; his village made out quite well with barter, when communal sharing didn't suffice. All the same, his uncle Regran had insisted that he bring along what few coins the village had.

Wuller dug them out and displayed them—a piece and three bits, in iron.

The proprietor snorted. "Damn peasants! Look, that'll buy you a heel of bread and let you sleep in the stable—anything more than that costs copper."

Old stories percolated in the back of his mind. "I could work," Wuller offered.

"I don't need any help, thank you," the innkeeper said. "You take your bread, get your water from the fountain, and you be out of here first thing in the morning."

Wuller nodded, unsure what to say. "Thank you" seemed more than the man deserved.

Then he remembered his mission. "Oh, wait!" he said, reaching back to pull out the sketch. "I'm looking for someone. Have you seen her?"

The innkeeper took the drawing and studied it, holding it up to the light.

"Pretty," he remarked. "And nicely drawn, too. Never saw her before, though—she certainly hasn't come through here *this* year." He handed the portrait back. "What happened, boy—your girl run away?"

"No," Wuller said, suddenly reluctant to explain. "It's a long story."

"Fine," the innkeeper said, turning away. "It's none of my business in any case."

9.

Wuller was gone the next morning, headed south, but not before listening to the chatter in the inn's common room and asking a few discreet questions when the opportunity arose.

He knew now that he was well inside the borders of the Baronies of Sardiron, that this inn, the Burning Pine, was the last before the border on the road north to Srigmor. Each spring and summer traders would head north, bringing the Srigmorites salt, spices, tools, and other things; each summer and fall they would come back home to Sardiron with wool, furs, and amber.

To the east lay The Passes, where a person could safely cross the mountains into the Valley of Tazmor, that fabulous realm that Wuller had never entirely believed in before.

There was little magic to be found around here, save for the usual village herbalists and a few primitive sorcerers and witches—but a mere fifteen leagues to the south was Sardiron of the Waters, where any number of magicians dwelt.

None of the people who had visited the inn had recognized the girl in the picture, or had any useful suggestions about finding her.

He also knew now that a lump of stale bread was not enough to still the growling of his stomach or stop the pinching he felt there, but that he could buy no better unless he could acquire some money—*real* money, copper or silver or even gold, not the cheap iron coins the peasants used among themselves.

As he left the village he sighed, and decided he needed to catch another squirrel or two—which would probably be a great deal more difficult now that he was in inhabited country.

Even as he decided this, he looked down the road ahead, past the trees on either side, and saw what looked like a very large clearing. He sighed again; squirrels preferred trees.

He watched both sides of the road carefully, but had spotted no game when he emerged into the "clearing" and realized his mistake.

This was no clearing. This was the edge of the forest.

Before him lay a vast expanse of open land, such as he had never seen before, or even imagined. Rolling hills stretched to the horizon covered with brown plowed fields and green grass, and dotted with farmhouses and barns. The highway drew a long, gentle curve across this landscape, no longer hidden by the forest gloom.

A few trees grew on the farms and hills, to be sure—shade trees sheltered some of the houses, and small groves of fruit trees or nut trees added some variety. In some places, neat lines of young trees marked boundaries between farms.

Most of the land was treeless, however, like the mountains where the sheep grazed above his home village.

He would find no squirrels here, he was sure.

Even as he came to that conclusion a rabbit leapt from concealment and dashed across the road in front of him, and he smiled. Where there was one rabbit, there would be others.

Two hours later he knocked on the door of a farmhouse by the roadside, a freshly-skinned rabbit in hand.

In exchange for half the rabbit and all of its fur, he was permitted to cook over the kitchen fire and eat sitting at the table, chatting with his hostess while two cats and three young children played underfoot. Water from the farmer's well washed the meal down nicely.

Thus refreshed, he set out southward again.

Not long after that he passed through a fair-sized town—to him, it seemed impossibly large and bustling, but he knew it couldn't be any place he had ever heard of, since he was still well to the north of Sardiron of the Waters. A large stone structure stood atop a hill to the east, brooding over the town and a highway, and Wuller realized with a shock that that big ugly thing was a castle.

Having no money, Wuller marched directly through without stopping.

An hour later he encountered another village, and another one an hour or so after that, though these had no castles. They had inns—but Wuller had no money.

At sunset, he found himself on the outskirts of another town. Like the village of the Burning Pine and the town with the castle, this one had three highways leaving it, rather than just two. Unlike the other towns, here the directions weren't north, south, and east, but north, south, and northeast; it wasn't a crossroads, but a fork.

There were no fewer than three inns on the town square; Wuller marvelled at that.

He was tired and hungry, so he did more than marvel—he went to each in turn and asked if he could work for a meal and a bed.

The proprietor of the Broken Sword said no, but was polite. The owner of the Golden Kettle threw him out. And at the Blue Swan the innkeeper's daughter took pity on him and let him clean the stables in exchange for bread, cheese, ale, and whatever he could pick off the bones when the paying customers were finished with their dinners.

She also found him a bed for the night—her own.

10.

No one at the Blue Swan could identify the girl in the portrait, but the innkeeper's daughter suggested he contact Senesson the Mage when he reached Sardiron itself. Senesson was a wizard who was said to be good at this sort of work.

There were a good many magicians of various sorts in her town of Keron-Vir, but she doubted any of them could help—and certainly not for free.

Wuller hesitated over that, but in the end he took her advice. After all, Sardiron of the Waters was only one day's walk away now, and he wanted to see the capital after coming so close. Besides, Teneria surely knew her own townspeople well enough to judge such things.

He did, however, stop in at the Golden Kettle and the Broken Sword to show the portrait around.

As he had expected, nobody knew who the girl in the picture was.

He shrugged, gathered his things, and set out.

He glimpsed the castle towers by mid-afternoon, and he could see the city walls and hear the thunder of the falls before the sun had set, but it was full dark by the time he reached the gates, with neither moon in the sky, and he made his entrance into Sardiron of the Waters by torchlight.

Even in the dark, he was impressed by the place. All the streets were paved with brick, flags, or cobbles—not a one was bare earth, anywhere inside the walls. Where the hillside was steep, the streets were built in steps, like a gigantic staircase.

The buildings were built up against each other, with no gap at all between them in many cases, while others left only a narrow alley—and even these alleys were paved.

Torches blazed at every intersection, and despite the gloom the streets were not deserted at all—people were going about their business even in the dark of night!

The sound was also amazing. The roar of the river was a constant background to everything, and fountains splashed in a dozen little squares and plazas, as well, as the city lived up to its name. A steady wind moaned endlessly around the black stone towers. On top of this were the normal sounds of a big, busy town—creaking cartwheels, lowing oxen, and a myriad of human voices chattering away.

The great castle of the Council of Barons reared up above the city, high atop the hill, looming darkly over everything.

The place was really like another world entirely, Wuller thought, as he looked about in confusion, wondering where he could eat or sleep.

A torchlit signboard caught his eye. There were no runes, but a faded painting of a dragon hatching from an egg.

That, he knew, must be an inn. And perhaps the dragon emblem was an omen, of sorts.

There was no broad window displaying ale kegs and pewter tankards, nor open door spilling light into the street, as there had been at the village inns he had seen so far—in fact, the only window here was a small one with bars on it, high above the street, and heavily curtained with black velvet. The only door was painted in four triangular sections, red at top and bottom and blue at either side, and studded with short spikes of black iron. It was tightly closed.

However, most of the city's architecture was equally strange and forbidding. He had seen no open doors or large windows *anywhere* inside the gates. This *had* to be an inn. He gathered his courage and knocked on the heavy wooden door, between the protruding spikes.

One of the spikes twisted, then slid back into the door and vanished; startled, Wuller looked into the hole it had left and saw an eye staring back at him.

Then the spike was replaced and the door swung open.

"We've no beds left," the old woman who had opened it announced, before he could say a word, "but if you've money for drink, we have plenty on hand."

"I don't have any money," Wuller explained, "but I'd be glad to work for a drink, or a bite to eat, or to sleep in a corner—I don't need a bed." He looked past her, into the common room, where a crowd of people was laughing and eating at tables set around a blazing hearth.

"We don't need any," the old woman began.

Wuller's gasp of astonishment interrupted her.

"Wait!" he said. "Wait!" He slid his pack off his shoulder and began digging through it.

"Young man," the woman said, "I don't have time for any nonsense..."

Wuller waved a hand at her. "No, wait!" he said. "Let me show you!" He pulled out the charcoal portrait and unrolled it.

"Lady, I've come all the way from northern Srigmor," Wuller explained, "on an errand for my village—there's a dragon, and...well, you don't care about that. But look!" He showed her the picture.

She took it and held it up to the light from the commons.

"Seldis of Aldagmor," she said. "Good likeness, too." She glanced into the room beyond, where the young woman Wuller sought was sitting alone at a table eating dinner, then looked at the picture again, and from the portrait back to Wuller. "What do you have to do with her?"

Wuller decided quickly that this was not the time for the complete and exact truth, but for something simpler.

"I must speak with her," he said. "The seer in our village knew her face, but not her name, and sent me to find her. I had thought I would have to search for sixnights yet, or months—but there she is in your dining hall! Please, let me come in and speak with her!"

The old woman looked at the portrait again, then turned to look at the young woman in the room beyond, sitting alone at a small table. Then she shrugged, and handed the picture back to Wuller.

"No business of mine," she said. "You behave yourself, though—any trouble and I'll have the guard in here."

"No trouble, lady," Wuller said. "I promise!"

11.

He settled into the chair opposite her, still astonished at his incredible good fortune, and astonished as well at her beauty. Neither Illuré's charcoal sketch nor the image in the oracle had really captured it.

"Hello," he said. "My name's Wuller Wulran's son."

She looked up from her plate and stared at him, but said nothing. The face was unmistakably the one he had seen in Kirna's oracle, the one that Illuré had drawn, with the vivid green eyes and the soft curls of dark brown hair. It was somewhat eerie to see it there in front of him as a real face, a small smudge of grease on the chin, rather than as a mere image.

The reality was more beautiful than the image, grease-spot notwithstanding.

"I've been looking for you," he said.

She turned her attention back to her plate, where a few fried potato slices remained. Wuller glanced at them, reminded how hungry he was, then returned his gaze to the top of her head.

"No, really, I've come all the way from northern Srigmor looking for you. My village elders sent me." He pulled out the portrait and unrolled it. "See?"

She raised her head, put a slice of potato in her mouth, and began chewing. She blinked. Then she put down her fork, reached out, and took the picture.

She stared at it for a moment, then looked at Wuller. "Did you do this, just now?" she asked. "It's pretty good."

"No," Wuller said. "My Aunt Illuré drew it, more than a sixnight ago."

"A sixnight ago I was home in Aldagmor," the girl said, her gaze wary.

"I know," Wuller said. "I mean, no, I didn't know at all, really, but I know that Illuré didn't see you. I mean, didn't *really* see you."

"Then how…all right, then who's this Illuré person? How did she draw this? I don't know anybody named Illuré that I can recall."

"You've never met her. She's my aunt, back home in Srigmor. She drew this because she's the best artist of the people who saw your face in the oracle."

"*What* oracle?"

"Kirna's family oracle."

"Who's Kirna?"

"She's one of the village elders. Her family got this sorcerer's oracle during the Great War, and it was passed down ever since, and when the dragon came…"

"What dragon? One of…I mean, what dragon?"

"The dragon that's captured my village."

The girl stared at Wuller for a moment, and then sighed. "I think you'd better start at the beginning," she said, "and explain the whole thing."

Wuller nodded, and took a deep breath, and began.

He described the dragon, how it had arrived one day without warning. He told her how it had killed Adar the Smith and given the village an ultimatum. He explained about the meeting in Kirna's hut, and how the oracle had shattered after showing them her face.

"…and they sent me to find you," he said. "And here I am, and I thought I'd have to find some way to hire a magician to find you, only I don't have any money, and then by sheer luck, here you are!"

"No money?" she asked.

"No," he said.

"Does *anyone* in your village have any money?"

"Not any more," he said, a trifle worried by this line of questioning.

He considered what he might do if she proved reluctant to come to the aid of the village. Small as he was for his age, he was still slightly bigger and stronger than she was; if worst came to worst, perhaps he could kidnap her and carry her home by force.

He hoped it wouldn't come to that. "Will you help?" he asked.

She looked down at the portrait she still held.

"Well," she admitted, "your oracle wasn't *completely* silly. I do know something about dragons. My family—well, my father's a dragon-hunter. That's been the family business for a long, long time now. That's why I come to this particular inn when I'm here, the Dragon's Egg, because of the connection with dragons. I was here in the city selling the blood from my father's latest kill to the local wizards; they use it in their spells. And some of my uncles will get rid of dragons when they cause trouble. But ordinarily…" She frowned. "Ordinarily, we don't work for free. This dragon of yours doesn't sound like one I've heard of before, so there's no question of family responsibility—I mean, this isn't one that we taught to talk, or anything. At least, I don't *think* it is."

Wuller suggested desperately, "We could pay in sheep, or wool."

She waved that away. "How would I get sheep from Srigmor to Aldagmor? Even if they made the trip alive, I'd do better just buying them at home. Same for wool. We don't raise as much in Aldagmor as you do up north, but we have enough."

"If you don't come, though," Wuller said, "my village will die. Even if the dragon doesn't eat us, we'll starve when the sheep are gone."

She drew a deep sigh. "I know," she said. She looked around the room, as if hoping that someone else would suggest a solution, but nobody else was listening.

"Well," she said, "I suppose I'll have to go."

Wuller couldn't repress his smile; he beamed at her.

"But I don't like it," she added.

12.

When she realized that he was not merely poor but totally penniless she bought him dinner, and allowed him to stay the night in her room at the inn. Wuller slept on the floor, and she slept on the bed, and he dared not suggest otherwise, either by word or deed.

For one thing, he had noticed that she carried a good long dagger in her belt, under the long vest she wore. The hilt was worn, which implied that it had seen much use and was not there simply for show.

In the morning she bought them both breakfast, gave the innkeeper a message to be sent to her father when next someone was bound to Aldagmor, bundled up her belongings, and stood waiting impatiently by the door while Wuller finished his meal and got his own pack squared away.

That done, the two of them marched side by side down the sloping streets toward the city gates. It had rained heavily during the night, and the cobbles were still damp and slippery, so that they had to move carefully.

This was the first time Wuller had seen Sardiron of the Waters by daylight, and he was too busy marveling at the strange buildings of dark stone, the fountains everywhere, the broad expanse of the river and the falls sparkling in the morning sun, to pay much attention to his beautiful companion.

Once they were out the gate, though, he found his gaze coming back to her often. She was very beautiful indeed. He had never seen another girl or woman to equal her.

He guessed her to be a year or two older than his own sixteen winters. Her face was too perfect to be much older than that, he thought, but she had a poise and self-assurance that he had rarely seen in anyone, of any age.

Although her beauty had been obvious, she had seemed less impressive, somehow, the night before; perhaps the dim light had been responsible. After all, as the saying had it, candlelight hides many flaws. Could it not equally well conceal perfection?

By the time they were out of earshot of the falls, and the towers of the council castle were shrinking behind them, he worked up the nerve to speak to her again for the first time since they had left the inn.

"You're from Aldagmor?" he asked.

Immediately, he silently cursed himself for such a banality. Where else could someone named Seldis of Aldagmor be from?

She nodded.

"Do you come here often, then?"

She looked at him, startled. "*Here*?" she asked, waving at the muddy highway and the surrounding farms. "I've never been *here* in my life!"

"I meant Sardiron," he said.

"Aldagmor's part of Sardiron," she replied. "Our baron's vice-chairman of the Council, in fact."

"I meant the *city*, Sardiron of the Waters," Wuller explained with a trace of desperation.

"Oh," she said. "Well, that's not *here*. We left the city hours ago." This was a gross exaggeration, but Wuller did not correct her. "I come down to the city about twice a year—usually once in the spring and once in the fall. I'm the one they can best spare, since I'm female and not strong enough for most of the work around…at home, so I make the trip to sell blood and hide and scales and order any supplies we need."

"Lucky we were there at the same time, then," Wuller said, smiling.

"Lucky for *you*," she said.

Wuller's smile vanished, and the conversation languished for a time.

The clouds thickened, and by midday it was drizzling. They stopped at an inn for lunch, hoping it would clear while they ate. Seldis paid for them both.

"This could be expensive," she remarked.

Wuller groped for something to say.

"We'll do our best to find a way to repay you," he said at last.

She waved it away. "Don't worry about it; it was my decision to come."

Two hours later, when they were on the road again and the rain had worked itself up into a heavy spring downpour, she snapped at him, "I don't know why I let you talk me into this!"

He said nothing.

13.

They stayed the first night at the Blue Swan, in the town of Keron-Vir, but this time Teneria the innkeeper's daughter was much less cooperative. She took one look at Seldis, and despite the dripping hair and soaked clothing saw that this was a beauty she could not possibly match; she refused to talk to either of them after that.

Seldis once again paid for meals and a small room, and once again she slept in the bed while Wuller slept on the floor.

He lay awake for half an hour or so, listening to the rain dripping from the eaves, before finally dozing off. He dared not even look at Seldis.

The rain had stopped by the time they left the next morning, and by noon Seldis was once again willing to treat Wuller as a human being. After a few polite remarks, he asked, "So how will you get rid of the dragon?"

"I don't know," she said, shrugging. "I'll need to see what the situation is."

"But—" he began.

She held up a hand. "No, really," she said, "I don't know yet, and even if I did, I might not want to tell you. Trade secrets, you know—family secrets."

Wuller did not press the matter, but he worried about it. The oracle had said that Seldis could rid the village of the dragon, and Seldis herself seemed confident of her abilities, but still, he worried.

He remembered Alasha's words, about virgins sacrificing themselves, and shifted his pack uneasily. Would Seldis sacrifice herself to the dragon?

The idea seemed silly at first thought—she hardly looked suicidal. On the other hand, she had agreed to make the journey in the first place, which certainly wasn't a selfish decision. Just how altruistic was she?

He stole a glance at her. She was striding along comfortably, watching a distant hawk circling on the wind—scarcely the image he would expect of someone who intended to fling herself into a dragon's jaws for the good of others.

He shook his head slightly. No, he told himself, that couldn't be what she intended.

A nagging thought still tugged at him, though—it might turn out to be what the *oracle* had intended.

They stayed that night at the Burning Pine, in the village of Laskros, and as Wuller lay on the floor of their room, staring at the plank ceiling, he wondered if he was doing the right thing by taking Seldis to his village.

Why should she risk going there?

Why should *he* risk going back?

Wouldn't it be better for both of them if they forgot about the dragon and the village and went off somewhere—Aldagmor, perhaps—together? He would court her, as best he could with no money and no prospects and no family…

No family. That was the sticking point. His family was waiting for him back home, relying on him. He couldn't let them down without even *trying*. Here he had had the phenomenal good luck to find his quarry quickly, as if by magic, and now he was considering giving up?

No, he had to go home, and to take Seldis with him, and then to help in whatever it took to dispose of the dragon.

He looked at her, lying asleep on the bed, her skin pale as milk in the light of the two moons, and then he rolled over and forced himself to go to sleep.

14.

"We won't be staying in inns after this," he told her the next morning. "We should leave the highway late today and go cross-country."

She turned to stare at him. "I thought you said it was another few days," she said.

"It is," he replied.

She glanced eastward, at the forests that now lined that side of the road.

"If you headed east for two days, anywhere along this road, you'd wind up in the mountains," she said. "Three days, and you'd be on bare stone, wouldn't you?"

"If you headed due east," he agreed. "But I didn't say that. We head north-northeast."

"For three or four days, you said?"

He nodded.

"Why not follow the road until we're ready to turn east, then? We'll be almost paralleling it!"

"Because," he said reluctantly, "I don't know the way if we do that. I can only find my way home by following the trail of peeled branches I marked coming south."

"Oh," she said.

A few paces later she asked, "What were you planning to eat, if we're leaving the road?"

He stopped dead in his tracks. "I hadn't thought of that," he admitted.

Seldis stared at him with an unreadable expression. "What did you eat on the way down?" she inquired.

"Squirrels, mostly," he said.

She sighed. "I think," she said, "that we had best go back to the Burning Pine and buy some provisions. With more of *my* money, of course."

Shame-faced, he agreed, and they retraced their steps.

When they reached Laskros Wuller pointed out a bakery and a smokeshop, so they did not in fact return to the Burning Pine for food. They did, however, buy three more blankets there. Wuller was proud of himself for thinking of that, and thought it partly compensated for his earlier foolishness.

There were no other delays, but the shopping expedition was enough to force them to sleep by the roadside that night, without having left the highway. Wuller refused to travel after the light began to fade, for fear of missing his trail, so the two of them settled down a dozen yards from the road, built a fire, and ate a leisurely dinner of sweet rolls and smoked mutton.

They chatted quietly about trivial matters—friends and family, favorite tales, and the like, never mentioning dragons or anything else unpleasant. When they were tired, they curled up in their separate blankets and went to sleep.

The next day they proceeded slowly, watching for marks, and at mid-morning or slightly thereafter Wuller spotted a pine branch with the bark curled back on the top—the mark he had used.

Standing under that branch he could see the next, and from that one the next.

Retracing his steps from tree to tree, they left the road and headed cross-country, back toward his home village.

They slept two more nights in the forest, but late the following afternoon Wuller recognized the landscape beyond any question, and a moment later Seldis spotted smoke from the village fires drifting above the trees.

They waited, and crept into the village under cover of darkness, making their way silently to Wuller's own home.

When Wuller swung the door inward he heard his father bellow, "Who the hell is it at this hour?"

He peered around the door and said, "It's me, Wuller. I'm back."

Wulran was speechless. He stared silently as Wuller stepped inside, and as Wuller then gave Seldis a helping hand up the stoop.

The two travelers dropped their packs to the floor. Wuller pointed out a chair to Seldis, who settled into it gratefully and then put her tired feet up on another.

"You can sleep in Aunt Illuré's room, I guess," Wuller told her. He turned back to his father for confirmation, and was astonished to see old Wulran weeping silently, tears dripping down his beard on either side.

15.

Wuller and Seldis arose late and spent the morning resting, soaking their tired feet and generally recovering from their journey. Meanwhile, Wuller's family scurried about the village, passing the word of his return and his success in finding the girl the oracle had shown them. A council meeting was called for that evening to discuss the next step.

Shortly after lunch, while Illuré was showing Seldis around the village, Wulran gestured for Wuller to come sit by him.

The lad obeyed, a trife warily.

"Wuller," the old man whispered, "you know what Alasha thinks, don't you?"

"About what?" Wuller asked.

"About this girl you brought back—about how she's to rid us of the dragon."

Wuller thought he knew what his father meant, but he hesitated before saying anything.

"She's to be a sacrifice," Wulran said. "That's what Alasha thinks. We may have to feed her to the dragon."

Wuller's thoughts were turbulent; he struggled to direct them enough to get words out, and failed.

"It's necessary," Wulran said. "Give up one life, and a foreigner at that, so that we all can live."

"We don't know that," Wuller protested. "We don't know if it's necessary or not!"

Wulran shrugged. "True," he said, "we don't know for sure, but can you think of any other way that fragile little thing could rid us of the dragon?"

Wuller didn't answer at first, because in truth, he could not. At last he managed, weakly, "She knows tricks, family secrets."

"She may know the ritual of sacrifice, I suppose," Wulran said.

Wuller could stand no more; he rose and marched off.

Wulran watched him go, and was satisfied when he saw that his son was not immediately heading off in search of the Aldagmorite girl, to warn her of her fate.

Wuller wanted to think before he did anything rash. He looked up at the mountaintop, where the dragon was sunning itself, and then around at the village, where his kin were all busily going about their everyday business. The sheep were out on the upslope meadows, and the smith's forge was quiet, the fires banked, but villagers were hauling water, or stacking firewood, or sitting on benches carding wool. To the west of the smithy, the downwind side, a hardwood rick was being burnt down for charcoal.

He pulled the rather battered charcoal portrait out of his sleeve and looked at it.

Seldis' face looked back at him.

He rolled the picture up and stuffed it back in his sleeve. Then he looked around.

Illuré and Seldis had been down to the stream, and were returning with buckets of water. Wuller thought about running over to them and snatching Seldis away, heading back south with her, away from the village—but he didn't move. He stood and watched as she and Illuré brought their pails to the cistern and dumped them in.

Seldis was not stupid enough to have come all this way just to die, he told himself. She surely knew what she was doing. She would have some way to kill the dragon, some magical trade secret her father had taught her.

At least, he hoped so.

16.

As the villagers gathered in Wulran's main room, that worthy pulled his son aside and whispered, "We'll listen to what the girl has to say, but then we may need to get her out of here for awhile. You understand. If that happens, you take her out and make sure she can't overhear anything. Later on we'll let you know where to bring her."

Wuller nodded unhappily, then took a seat in the corner.

He understood perfectly. He was to be the traitor ram who would lead Seldis to the slaughter, if it came to that.

A few minutes later Wulran closed the door and announced, "I think everybody's here."

A sudden expectant silence fell as the quiet chatter died away.

"I think you all know what's happened," Wulran said. "My son Wuller went south to find the girl the oracle showed us, and damn me if he didn't find her and bring her back, all in less than a month. The gods must like us, to make it as easy as that!"

He smiled broadly, and several polite smiles appeared in response.

"She's here now," he continued, "so let's bring her on out and get down to business!" He waved to Illuré, who led Seldis to the center of the room.

A murmur ran through the gathering at the sight of her.

"I am Seldis of Aldagmor," the girl announced. Several people looked startled, as if, Wuller thought, they hadn't expected her to talk. They had been thinking of her as a thing, rather than a person, he guessed—the easier to sacrifice her to the dragon.

Wuller suppressed a growl at the thought. What good would sacrificing anybody do?

"My family has fought and killed dragons since the days of the Great War," Seldis continued, "and I think I ought to be able to rid you of this one. First, though, I need to know everything about it, and what you've already tried. Wuller Wulran's son told me a little on the journey up here from Sardiron, but I need to know everything."

Several voices spoke up in reply, but after a moment's confusion matters straightened themselves out. Kirna told the tale of the dragon's arrival and the death of Adar the Smith, and of the ancient sorcerous oracle and the image it had shown them. Her sister Alasha corrected her on various details, and Wulran interjected commentary as he thought appropriate.

Seldis listened, and asked a question every so often—did the dragon seem to favor one side over the other when it ripped the smith apart, or did it use both foreclaws equally? Was its flight steady, like a hawk's, or did it bob slightly, like a crow?

"...so we all agreed that Wuller should go, and the next morning he did," Kirna concluded, "while we all waited here. From there on, lady, you know better than we."

Seldis nodded. "And what did you do while you waited?" she asked.

The villagers looked at her and at one another in surprise.

"Nothing," Alasha said. "We just waited."

Seldis blinked. "You didn't try anything else?" she asked.

Several people shook their heads.

"And you hadn't tried anything else before you talked to this oracle?"

"No," Kirna said. "What could we try? We saw what it did to Adar!"

Seldis stared around at the gathered villagers, and Wuller knew that she was trying hard to conceal genuine astonishment.

What had she *expected* them to try, he wondered.

Seldis closed her lips into a thin line, and then said, "Well, you haven't been very much help, not having tried anything, but I certainly know what I'm going to try first. I can't believe none of you ever thought to try it. You feed the beast a sheep every day, don't you?"

Heads nodded, and Wulran said, "Yes."

"Then I'll need about two dozen little pouches," Seldis said. "Pigs' bladders would be perfect. I didn't see many pigs around, though, so sheep bladders would do. Sausage casing should work, or even leather purses, if they're sewn very tightly. They need to be small enough to stuff down a sheep's throat—but not too small, and it doesn't matter if it hurts the sheep."

A confused murmur ran through the room.

Wuller blinked, puzzled. He glanced at his father in time to see Wulran giving him a meaningful stare and making a wiggling gesture with one finger.

His father thought Seldis was mad, he realized.

He rebelled mentally at that. He had spent a sixnight with her, and he knew she was not mad. Whatever she intended to do had to be a dragonhunter's trick, not a madwoman's folly.

And whatever it was, he would help her with it.

17.

The meeting broke up quickly after that. Seldis refused to explain what she had in mind. Most of the people didn't seem to think she really had *anything* in mind, but everyone agreed to let her have a day to make her attempt.

Wulran managed another surreptitious chat with his son, and made it quite clear to Wuller that it was his duty to keep an eye on Seldis and make sure she didn't slip away.

Wuller agreed, unhappily, not to let her out of his sight.

After breakfast the next morning Seldis rose from the table, stretched, and said, "I'm going for a walk to gather some herbs. Could someone lend me a basket? A big one?"

Illuré produced one that Seldis found suitable, and the three of them, Seldis, Illuré, and Wuller, strolled out into the woods beyond the village.

They walked for several minutes in companionable silence, enjoying the warm spring weather. Wuller glanced at Illuré, and then at Seldis, and then back at his aunt.

He had no desire to play traitor ram. If he could get Seldis away from Illuré he would warn her what the elders had in mind, and give her a chance to slip away.

Just then Seldis said, "I don't see what I'm looking for anywhere. Illuré, where can I find wolfsbane or nightshade around here?"

"Find what?" Illuré said, startled. "I never heard of those; what are they?"

Seldis looked at Illuré, equally startled. "Why, they're plants, fairly common ones. Wolfsbane has little flowers with hoods on them; on the sort that would be blooming at this time of year the blossoms are yellow and very small, but the other kinds can have blue or purple or white flowers."

"I never heard of it," Illuré said, "and I don't think I've ever seen it. Are you sure it grows around here?"

"Maybe not," Seldis said, her expression worried. "What about nightshade?"

"What is it?" Illuré asked.

Seldis said, "Well, it's got flowers like little bells, dark red ones, and little black berries."

Illuré stood and puzzled for a moment.

"I don't think we have that, either," she said at last. "If you want flowers, we have daisies."

"No, I don't want flowers!" Seldis snapped.

"Well, then, what *do* you want?" Illuré asked.

"Never mind. Let's just go back." She turned and headed toward the village.

Wuller and Illuré followed her, baffled.

Wuller glanced at Illuré, wondering if this might be the best chance they would have for Seldis to slip away, but then he decided to wait. The Aldagmorite seemed far more worried than she had earlier, but still not frightened; Wuller thought she must still have something in mind, even without her magical herbs.

In the village they found Wulran glowering at them from his doorstep, and Kirna sitting nearby with a basket full of sausage casings. Other villagers were watching from a safe distance.

"Will these do?" Kirna asked, displaying her basket.

Seldis shook her head. "Those would be perfect," she said, "but I'm afraid my idea won't work. I couldn't find what I needed. I guess I'll have to think of something else."

Wulran snorted. "Lady," he said, "I guess you will, and quickly. The oracle said you could save us from the dragon, but you won't do it by wandering the hills, and we can't risk your wandering off completely. From now on, you'll stay here, in the village, under guard."

"But..." Seldis began.

"No argument!" Wulran shouted. The other villagers murmured.

Seldis didn't argue. At Wulran's direction, she was led into the house and sent into Illuré's room, where new brackets were set on either side of the door, and a bar placed across.

The window, too, was barred, and Seldis was a prisoner.

Wuller, quite involuntarily, found himself appointed her gaoler.

"She's mad, and the mad are dangerous," his father explained, out of her hearing, "but she trusts you. She'll stay if you guard her. If she can tell us how to kill the dragon, all well and good, but if she can't then we'll put her out as tomorrow's sacrifice. That must be what the oracle intended in the first place."

Wuller didn't try to argue. He knew Seldis was not mad, but he had no idea what she had been planning, and also saw that his father was frightened and angry and would brook no discussion.

Something would have to be done, of course, but not with words.

Wuller settled down at the door to Seldis' improvised cell and waited.

Early in the afternoon, when everyone else had grown bored and left, he called in to her, "What's so special about those plants you wanted?"

"Am I allowed to speak now, then?" she asked sarcastically.

"Of course you are. Listen, I'm very sorry about all this; it's not *my* fault!"

"Oh, I know, but it's so *stupid*! There's nothing magical about dragon-killing; it's easy, if you put a little thought into it. Everyone around here is just too scared to *think*! What good does it do to lock me up like this?"

"It keeps you from running away," Wuller said, a bit hesitantly.

"But that's idiotic. After walking all the way up here, why would I run away now?"

"Because..." Wuller began, and then stopped.

If she didn't already know she was to be sacrificed, would it do any good to tell her?

Maybe not.

"Never mind that for now," he said instead. "What's so special about those plants?"

"They're poisonous. Wuller, what are you hiding? What are they...oh, no. They aren't really *that* stupid and superstitious, are they? A maiden sacrifice, is that what they're planning?"

Wuller didn't answer. Her answer to his question had brought sudden comprehension. He thought for a moment, and saw it all—not merely what Seldis had originally planned, but what they could do instead.

"Wuller? Are you there?" she called through the door.

"I'm here," he said, "and don't worry. Just wait until tonight. Trust me."

"*Trust* you?" She laughed bitterly.

18.

When Wuller brought in her dinner Seldis refused to speak to him; she glared silently, and after a muttered apology he didn't press it.

Later, though, when the others were all asleep, he carefully unbarred the door, moving slowly to avoid making noise or bumping anything with the heavy bar.

"Come on," he whispered.

She stepped out quickly. "Where?" she asked. "Are you just letting me go?"

He shook his head. "No, no," he said, "we're going to kill the dragon, just as you planned. I've got a sheep tied outside, and Kirna left the basket of sausage casings; everything's ready."

"You found wolfsbane? Or nightshade?"

"No," he said. "Those don't grow around here."

Seldis started to protest.

"Hush! It's all right, really. I know what I'm doing. Come on, and don't make any more noise!"

She came.

In the morning Wulran found his son sound asleep, leaning against the barred door of Illuré's bedroom. Wuller looked rather dirtier and more rumpled than Wulran remembered him being the night before, and Wulran looked the lad over suspiciously.

He hoped that Wuller hadn't gone and done anything stupid.

He wondered if there was anything to the stories about dragons demanding virgins for sacrifice.

How could a dragon tell, though?

More magic at work, presumably.

Whatever magic was involved, Wulran hoped that the girl was still in there to be sacrificed, and hadn't slipped out in the night. What if the boy's dirt came from chasing through the woods after her?

He poked Wuller with a toe. "Wake up," he said.

Wuller blinked and woke up. "Good morning," he said. Then he yawned and stretched.

"Is the girl still in there?" Wulran demanded.

Wuller looked at the door, still closed and barred, and then up at his father. "I think so," he said. "She was last I saw."

"And she'll be there when we come to get her for the sacrifice?"

Wuller yawned again. "You can't sacrifice her," he said. "I already fed the dragon this morning, just before first light. It's probably dead by now."

"What's probably dead by now, a sheep? You fed it a sheep?"

Wuller nodded. "Yes, I fed it a sheep, and of course the *sheep* is dead, but what I meant was, the *dragon* is probably dead."

His father stared at him.

"What?" he asked.

Wuller got to his feet.

"I said, the dragon is probably dead by now."

"Have you gone mad, too, now?" Wulran asked. "I didn't know it was catching."

"I'm not mad," Wuller said. He didn't like his father's tone, though, and he suddenly decided not to say any more.

"Step aside, boy," Wulran demanded. "I want to be sure she's in there."

Wuller stepped aside.

He said nothing as his father unbarred the door and found Seldis peacefully asleep in Illuré's bed.

He said nothing at all for the rest of the morning, not even when the men came later and found Seldis still sleeping, and picked her up and carried her off to the flat stone where the dragon took its meals.

19.

Seldis awoke the moment they laid hands on her, but she didn't scream or struggle. She put up no resistance as the party carried her to the flat, bloodstained stone outcropping where the dragon accepted its tribute.

There she was lowered gently to the ground. One end of a rope was tied around her ankles, the other to the tall scorched stump beside the stone where, prior to this, only sheep had been tethered. Her hands, too, were tied.

Then she was placed on the stone, and the others stepped back, leaving her there.

She looked up at the villagers and addressed Wuller directly. "You better be right about those mushrooms," she said.

He looked up at the mountainside above them, and smiled. "See for yourself," he said, pointing.

She looked where Wuller pointed, and saw the tip of the dragon's tail, hanging down from a ledge like an immense bloated vine. No one else had noticed; they had been paying attention to their captive.

The tail was utterly limp.

"See?" Wuller said. "It's dead, just as you said it would be."

The villagers looked, and then stared in open-mouthed astonishment.

"We'd better go make sure," Seldis said. "I'm not familiar with those mushrooms. If it's just sick, we'd better go finish it off while it's still weak."

"Right," Wuller said. He knelt beside her and drew his knife, then began sawing at the ropes.

Wulran tore his gaze from that dangling, lifeless tail and looked down at the bound young woman. "What did you *do*?" he asked.

"We killed the dragon, Wuller and I," she said. "I told you I knew how." Her wrists were free, and she sat up.

"But *how*?" Wulran asked.

"It was easy. Wuller let me out last night, and we went out in the woods and gathered mushrooms, two baskets full—those thin ones with the white stems and the little cups at the bottom. You don't have wolfsbane or nightshade around here, but you had to have *something* poisonous, and Wuller told me about the mushrooms."

"But how…" someone began.

Seldis ignored him and kept right on speaking.

“We ground up the mushrooms and stuffed them into those sausage casings, and then we stuffed *those* down the throat of a sheep Wuller brought, and then we tied the sheep here—oh, look, some of its blood got on my skirt! Didn’t you people see it was still wet?”

Wuller grinned at her as the rope around her ankles parted.

“Anyway,” Seldis continued, “we tied it out, and the dragon ate it, and that was that.”

“Poison mushrooms?” someone asked. “That’s all it took?”

“Of *course* that’s all!” Seldis said, plainly offended. “Do you think I’m an amateur? I know how to kill dragons, I told you!”

“You’re sure it’s dead?” Wulran asked. “I mean, I know those mushrooms are deadly, but that’s a *dragon…*”

Seldis shrugged. “A dragon’s just a beast. A very special beast, a magical beast perhaps, but a beast, of mortal flesh and blood. Poison will kill it, sure as it will kill anything.”

20.

“We need to check,” Wulran said gruffly. “We can’t just take your word for it that it’s dead.”

“You’re right,” Seldis said. “If I got the dose wrong it might just be sick for a few days. We need to go see, and if it’s still alive we need to finish it off while it’s weak.”

The villagers looked at one another.

“You don’t all have to go,” Seldis said. “Wuller and I will check.”

“I’ll come, too,” Wulran said.

“If you like. There’s one thing, though—could someone fetch me a wineskin, the biggest you can find?”

The villagers were puzzled, but none of them were inclined to argue with her any further.

Several minutes later, the three of them, Wulran, Wuller, and Seldis, set out up the mountainside to the ledge where the dragon's tail was draped. Seldis carried an immense empty wine-skin, the sort that would be hung up on the village commons during Festival, and still no one had had the nerve to ask her why.

They crept up onto the ledge, past the thick tail, and down into the stony crevice where most of the dragon lay, motionless and silent.

"It *looks* dead," Wuller whispered as they came even with the great belly.

Seldis nodded. "Looks can be deceiving, though." She took out her long knife and crept forward, toward the head.

"What are you…" Wuller began.

"Stay back!" she hissed. "I'm going to make sure it's dead."

Wulran reached out and grabbed Wuller's arm, and pulled him back to the edge of the ledge, where they could both slide down out of sight in a hurry if the need arose.

They waited for what seemed hours to Wuller, but watching the sun he realized it was only a few minutes.

"It's all right," Seldis called at last. "It's dead!"

Wuller ran back down the crevice after her, calling, "How can you be sure?"

Then he saw what she had done. She had rammed her long knife up to the hilt into one of the dragon's eyes.

If there had been any life in it at all, it would surely have reacted to that!

After that, she had swung her wineskin into position and cut open a vein, allowing the dragon's blood to spill into the waiting receptacle. Wuller stared at the trickle of purplish ichor.

"This will cover my expenses," she said, almost apologizing. "Wizards can always use more dragon's blood."

"It's really dead," Wuller said. "We did it! Seldis, we all owe you more than we could ever pay you, and particularly after the treatment you got. I'm sure that everyone in the village will agree with me on that."

Wulran came up behind him and said, "If they don't at first, I'll make them agree, young lady."

Seldis shrugged. "It's nothing. This one was easy. Hell, you people should have thought of it yourselves! You knew about the mushrooms, and you saw it eat a sheep every day—why didn't you try *anything*?"

Wulran shrugged. "We had that prophecy, that oracle—that you would come save us." He smiled crookedly.

Seldis stared at him.

"So you were going to sacrifice me?" she asked. "You thought that would save you?"

Wulran opened his mouth to reply, and then closed it again.

"Did it occur to any of you that if sacrificing me was *not* what the oracle had meant, that you'd be killing the one person who you'd been told could save you?"

Wulran merely blinked at that; he didn't even try to respond.

Wuller said, "I wouldn't have let them."

"Ha! I didn't see you doing much to stop them this morning!"

"But we'd already poisoned the dragon by then!"

"And what if the poison hadn't worked?"

Wuller's mouth opened, like his father's, but nothing came out.

Seldis looked at him for a long moment, then at the dragon. The stream of blood had stopped; she capped the wineskin and hung it over one shoulder. Then she shoved her way past both the son and the father and marched on out of the crevice.

Wulran and Wuller watched her go. Wulran threw his son an apologetic glance, but Wuller was in no mood to accept it. He ran after her.

When he caught up with her he could think of nothing to say, and so the two of them walked silently back down to the village side by side.

When they reached the village, Seldis announced, "I'm tired, Wuller; we were up all night. I'm going to get some sleep."

He nodded. "Good idea," he said.

After she had gone into Illuré's bedroom—leaving the door open and unbarred, this time—he headed for his own bed.

Wuller awoke that afternoon to find her up and dressed and checking her pack. The wineskin of dragon's blood was at her feet.

"I'll be going now," she said, without looking at him.

Wuller blinked at her from the doorway of his bedroom. He looked around at the familiar house—his mother's painted tiles on the walls, the iron skillets hung by the kitchen, the broad stone hearth. His parents and his aunt Illuré were somewhere nearby. Around the house stood his village, all the world he had known until a few days ago, home to his entire extended family and everyone he had ever known.

All of it was safe now, with the dragon dead, and Seldis was no longer needed. She would be going back to her own home, in distant Aldagmor, out there in the hostile and unfamiliar world beyond the village, the world where Wuller knew no one and had nothing.

"Wait for me," he said, snatching up his clothes.

To his surprise, she did.

ABOUT "NIGHT FLIGHT"

Mercedes Lackey invited me to contribute a story to an anthology of fantasy stories about birds of prey, and I hadn't written any Ethshar stories for awhile, so I wrote this one. I don't know much about hawks or eagles, but I do know owls, and I figured most of the other contributors wouldn't think of owls, or write from the prey's point of view.

NIGHT FLIGHT

Princess Kirna of Quonmor sat upon her bed and frowned at the barred window. The sun was down and daylight was fading rapidly; she would be spending another night here in the wizard's tower, and once again, she would be spending it locked in this room, all alone. This was not working out at all as she had expected.

Running off with a wizard had seemed like such a very romantic idea! She had thought she could entice him to either marry her, whereupon they would travel all over the World having wonderful adventures together, or to take her on as his apprentice, whereupon she would spend years learning all the secrets of magic and then someday return to Quonmor to find a usurper on the throne, whom she, as the rightful heir, would then depose and punish horribly for his effrontery. Her subjects would cheer as she crowned herself queen in her father's throne room, and she would use her magic to transform Quonmor into a paradise, and to reconquer Demmamor, which her great-grandfather had lost.

And then perhaps she would reunite all the Small Kingdoms into an empire—after all, if that warlock Vond could conquer a dozen of them, without having even a trace of royal blood, why couldn't a wizard-queen rule them all?

But this had all depended on this Gar of Uramor falling in love with her, or at least taking her seriously, and so far he hadn't. He hadn't objected to her company on the walk home, but when she had tried to flirt with him he had laughed and said she was too young, and when she had asked about an apprenticeship he had said she was too old.

When she had explained that she was a princess, so the ordinary rules didn't apply to her, he had gotten angry and locked her up here, in this room with the thick iron-bound door and the distressingly-solid iron bars in the window.

When he came back—well, it had been downright embarrassing. He had treated her as if she were little more than a baby, and hadn't agreed to *anything.* What was the good of being a princess if you couldn't have what you wanted?

She pouted, and bounced on the bed—it wasn't as soft as her featherbed at home, but it was pleasantly springy and fun to bounce on.

"Princess Kirna?" a breathy voice asked.

Startled, she stopped bouncing and smoothed out her face—her father had always told her a princess mustn't pout. The voice hadn't been Gar's. It had sounded as if it was right beside her, but of course there wasn't anyone else in the room; she turned toward the door and called, "Who is it?"

"Hush!" She jumped; the voice was right in her ear.

"Who's there?" she whispered.

A vague blue shape shimmered in the air before her, and the voice said, in slightly-accented Quonmoric, "I am Deru of the Nimble Fingers. I've come to help you." The blue shape raised a hand, and she glimpsed a blurry face.

"A ghost!" she gasped. "A real ghost!"

"No, I'm not a ghost," Deru said. "I'm a wizard under a spell."

She flung a hand up to cover her mouth. "You're under a *curse*? That terrible Gar did this to you, and is keeping you prisoner here?"

"No, no," Deru assured her. "I did it to myself, so I could get in here to talk to you. It's called the Cloak of Ethereality. It'll wear off soon."

"Oh," she said, disappointed. "You just came to talk to me?"

"I was sent to find out why you're here."

Kirna stared at the misty blue outline for a moment. Who *was* this person? Who had sent him? Was he really here at all?

He said he was a wizard—had the Wizards' Guild sent him?

Might Gar be in trouble? Kirna had heard stories about the dreadful things the Wizards' Guild did to people who broke its rules…

Maybe he wasn't in trouble yet, but he *could* be, and it would serve him right for mistreating her.

"He kidnapped me!" she said. "He dragged me here and locked me up, and he *tortured* me!" She held up her left hand, where Gar had nicked her with a knife to draw a vial of blood.

The apparition stooped to stare at her hand, and she snatched it away before he could see just how small the cut really was.

"He took my blood," she said. "I'm sure he's going to do something *terrible* with it."

"He took your blood," Deru said thoughtfully. "Anything else? Hair? Tears?"

She blinked at him, startled; this wasn't the reaction she had expected. She decided she had better tell the truth—more or less.

"Yes," she said. "He tortured me until I cried, then caught my tears with a cloth and a little jar." The "torture" had just been shouting and teasing, but she didn't see any need to admit that.

The misty figure nodded.

"Well, that'll be *some* relief to your father, anyway."

"That I was *tortured*?" Then she realized what he had said. "My father?"

Deru nodded. "Your parents sent me," he said. "Didn't I say that?"

"No, you didn't!" Kirna felt cheated; this ghostly figure hadn't come from the Wizards' Guild after all. Then she remembered the rest of the conversation. "You think they'll be relieved that I was *tortured*?"

"No, they'll be relieved that Gar was collecting your tears," he said. "Normal tears aren't worth anything, but a virgin's tears are used in at least half a dozen different spells. If Gar was collecting yours, then he didn't rape you."

Somehow Kirna found that annoying. "Yet," she said. "He still might, now that he's filled that jar!"

"I suppose he might, at that," Deru agreed. "Virgin's blood and hair and tears are all valuable, but so are various parts of unborn children."

Kirna's eyes widened in horror. "He wouldn't!"

"Well, people do," Deru said. "And if he kidnapped a princess, who knows what he might do? On the other hand, he might just keep you here and murder your parents—there are a few very powerful spells that call for the tears of a virgin *queen*, rather than just any virgin. Those spells are beyond my abilities, but maybe Gar knows them…"

Kirna shrieked. "*Murder* my *parents*?"

"The Guild wouldn't approve, but…"

"No! You need to stop him!"

"The easiest way for me to do that would be to take you home," Deru said. "I'm sure that if you were safely back at Quonmor Keep, with guards all around you, that he wouldn't bother—he'd find an easier target."

"Take me home!" Kirna said.

"I'd be glad to," Deru said. "The question is, how do we get you out of here? Do you think Gar would just let you go, if you asked?"

Kirna stared at him. "Haven't you heard anything I've told you?" she said. "He *kidnapped* me and *dragged* me here and locked me up and *tortured* me!"

Deru sighed. "But he might have just wanted the blood and tears. He's got those now, so maybe he'll let you go."

"You're crazy!" Kirna said. "He intends to keep me here forever, I'm *sure* of it!"

Actually, Gar had said something about sending her home in the morning, but she wasn't about to admit that. She had failed to impress Gar, but perhaps this other wizard, this Deru, might be more amenable. Perhaps, once they were out of this awful tower, she could convince him to run away with her, so they could marry and have adventures and he could teach her all his magic.

Maybe she could even get him to *kill* Gar! A wizards' duel, fought over her—she shivered with excitement at the thought.

Deru sighed. "Well, you're probably right. I'll just have to get you out of here without him knowing it."

"Oh." Her excitement dimmed. That meant no duel.

But still, it would be a dramatic rescue that might lead to romance.

"How?" she asked.

"Leave that to me," he said.

Then he vanished.

"*Hai*!" she called. "Where are you?"

No one answered.

* * * *

Deru stepped out through the locked door of the third-floor chamber, back out into the stairwell, ignoring Kirna's calls.

He suspected the princess was embellishing her story somewhat; he still didn't think Gar had brutally kidnapped her and dragged her away, as she alleged. The Wizards' Guild forbade its members to interfere with any sort of royal succession, and kidnapping a princess would qualify; Deru had trouble believing Gar would openly defy that rule. To do so was suicidal, and Gar didn't appear to be sufficiently deranged.

Besides, how could he have done it without being noticed—and without putting a single mark on her face? Deru had studied her briefly before becoming visible—he was in no hurry, since the Cloak of Ethereality lasted a predetermined length of time and he could not remove it for hours yet, so he had taken a few minutes to explore the tower and look over the princess. He hadn't seen a bruise or scratch anywhere on her, except for the one little incision on her hand.

But Gar *had* locked her in, and collected blood and tears and hair—and besides, it would make a much better story to carry out a magical rescue than to simply walk her home, and it would be easier to collect a huge fee if he had a good story to tell.

Deru drifted invisibly up the stairs to Gar's workshop, and peered in at his fellow wizard.

There was no need to do anything to Gar; he appeared to be settled in for the evening, and if Kirna disappeared he probably wouldn't notice anything until morning.

And when he *did* notice, he probably wouldn't do anything about it. After all, Kirna was Crown Princess of Quonmor, and the Wizards' Guild had rules against meddling with royalty. If Deru could just get the girl out of the tower, that should be the end of Gar's involvement. And after that, it was only twelve miles back to Quonmor Keep; that wouldn't be a difficult walk.

Deru looked past Gar at the open window; the cool outside air was stirring the curtains slightly, and the light of the greater moon tinted the white muslin orange. Somewhere in the forest outside the tower an owl hooted.

It all seemed peaceful enough. There was no point in being unnecessarily complicated; all he had to do was get Kirna out of the tower. He had come prepared for that—he had brought the materials he needed for Riyal's Transformation, and had even prepared the oakleaf-tea countercharm in advance.

He allowed himself to sink through the floor, back to Kirna's room, to wait for the Cloak's spell to break.

* * * *

There was no flash or bang; one moment Kirna was lying in bed, half-asleep but kept awake by wondering about her mysterious ghostly visitor, alone in her candle-lit room, and the next instant a curly-haired young man in a blue silk cloak was standing next to her, holding a finger to his lips.

Her eyes opened wide; she flung off the blanket and sat up. "You're back!" she said.

"Yes, I am," he said, his voice low. "And in a few hours we'll be out of here and on our way back to Quonmor."

"A few hours?"

"Yes," he said. "We'll be going out that window." He pointed.

"But it's barred," Kirna said. "Are you going to turn me into a ghost like you?"

He shook his head. "No, that spell only works on wizards, but I brought another that can affect us both. It will shrink us down until we can easily walk between those bars, and then I can levitate us safely down to the ground."

"*Shrink* us?"

He nodded. "We'll be not much larger than mice. It takes about three hours to prepare."

She hesitated. "Is it safe?"

"Oh, yes," Deru assured her. "It won't harm you, and the countercharm is very easy—just a drink of a special tea." He slipped a battered leather pack off his shoulder, opened the top flap, and pulled out a brown glass flask. "This is the cure right here—a sip of this will break the spell and restore you instantly to your normal size. Once we're well away from the tower we'll drink it, and then it's just a matter of walking you home."

"Oh," Kirna said.

This was exciting, in its way—the idea of being shrunk down to the size of a mouse was strange, certainly—but it wasn't quite what she had hoped for. Walking home? Not flying, or vanishing in a puff of smoke from one place and appearing with a flash in another? Shrunk down, but not turned into birds?

Well, it would do, and perhaps it would be more interesting than it sounded.

"Now, I need you to stay close, and stay quiet, while I prepare the spell," Deru said. "Oh, and you'll need to open the shutter and casement, so we can get out once we're small."

"All right," Kirna said. Rather than wait, she rose and opened the window immediately, while Deru removed and folded up his silken cloak and fished more items out of his pack.

Beneath the rather dramatic cloak he was wearing a disappointingly-ordinary brown-and-cream tunic and suede breeches. Kirna had hoped for something more wizardly.

A moment later, as she sat on the bed and watched, Deru began the ritual. He drew lines on the floor with something white and waxy, then positioned three candles on the resulting design before seating himself cross-legged at the center.

He lit the candles one by one while mumbling something Kirna could not make out, then set out a dagger, two scraps of fur, and two tiny, bright-red objects Kirna did not recognize. The mumbling turned into a rhythmic chanting, and his hands moved through the air in curious patterns.

Every so often he would lean over and move one of the objects, and sometimes he was holding a lump of the white stuff, sometimes he wasn't.

It was all very mysterious and magical—and after the first few minutes, boring. Kirna watched, waiting for something to happen, but the chant droned on endlessly…

She awoke with a start to find Deru standing over her, shaking her gently. "Your Highness!" he said. "Wake up!"

"I'm awake!" she said irritably, sitting up and looking at the room.

The air was thick and hot, and she had trouble seeing clearly, whether from sleep or smoke she was not sure. All the candles had burned out but one, which was down to a smoking stub; the design on the floor had vanished, but an identical design of white smoke hung in the air a foot above where it had been drawn. The dagger was sheathed and on Deru's belt, and the other things were gone.

Her head seemed to be buzzing, and she suddenly was unsure whether she was awake or dreaming or somewhere in between.

"Stick out your tongue," Deru said.

"What?" The unexpected order halfway convinced her she was dreaming.

"Stick out your tongue! Quickly! We need to do this before the candle goes out!"

Confused, Kirna stuck out her tongue, and Deru quickly pressed something onto it, a tiny something that tickled and scratched, and stuck.

"Wha..." She tried to talk, but the object on her tongue made it difficult; she gagged.

Deru was holding out a piece of fur; he reached over her shoulders with it, then stretched it out. She could feel it on her back, and it seemed to be stretching out forever.

"What's that?" she asked, and discovered that the thing on her tongue had dissolved away into nothingness. She looked up at Deru, who seemed to be taller suddenly. The ceiling was rising up away from her, as well.

"It's the skin of a field mouse," Deru said, as he wrapped it around her.

She tumbled from the bed, and it was a much longer fall than it should have been; she landed on her hands and knees, her palms stinging with the impact. Her vision blurred.

When it cleared again she clambered to her feet and looked up.

Deru stood before her, unspeakably huge, the pack on his shoulder the size of Quonmor Keep; between the gigantic pillars of his legs she could see the smoking stub of candle, taller than she was. The pattern of smoke hung over her, out of reach. She looked up, and up, and up.

Deru was putting a tiny red thing on his own tongue; that done, he took a scrap of gray fur and lifted his hands up over his head.

And then he began shrinking. The mouse-pelt didn't stretch; Deru shrank.

And moment later he stood before her at his normal height, a few inches taller than herself, as the candle flared up and went out and the pattern of smoke dissipated. Darkness descended, broken only by the orange glow of the greater moon outside the open window.

The little bedchamber stretched out before them in the dimness, an immensity of space.

"There," Deru said. "It worked."

"Oh," Kirna said, looking around.

The world was strange and different, with ordinary furniture become looming monstrosities, but she no longer suspected she was dreaming; everything was quite solid and real. She looked up at the window, impossibly far above them, and asked, "How do we get out?"

"We levitate. Or rather, I do. I'll have to carry you, I'm afraid; I don't have a levitation spell that will work on both of us."

She frowned, but could hardly argue. She was no wizard.

At least, not yet.

Deru knelt and opened his pack. He pulled out a small lantern, a grey feather, and a silver bit; he lit the lantern, set the coin inside it, then drew his dagger again and did something Kirna could not see. Then he straightened up, the lantern in his hand and the dagger back in his belt; the feather seemed to have vanished.

"Come here," he said.

Cautiously, Kirna approached—and then shrieked as Deru grabbed her and hoisted her over his shoulder, her head and arms dangling down his back, her legs pinned to his chest. She raised her head and turned to look around.

Deru was walking, one hand holding her legs and the other carrying the lantern—but he was not walking across the floor; instead he was walking up into the air, as if climbing an invisible staircase.

"Varen's Levitation," he said.

Kirna made a wordless strangled noise. She had wanted to learn magic and have adventures, but being shrunk to the size of a mouse, flung over someone's shoulder, and carried up into the air, with nothing at all holding them up, all in quick succession, was a little more than she had been ready for.

But, she told herself, she was being silly. This *was* a magical adventure! She should appreciate it.

She thought she could appreciate it much more easily if she weren't draped over Deru's shoulder, though. She tried to twist around for a better view.

"You don't want me to drop you," Deru cautioned. "The spell only works on me."

Kirna ignored that and watched. Deru was marching up higher and higher above the floor, and had now turned toward the window. Kirna could see the sky and the surrounding treetops, lit by the orange light of the greater moon—the feeble glow of the tiny lantern didn't reach more than a few inches.

Fitting between the bars would be no problem at all at their present size—but how would they get *down?*

"Shouldn't you have a rope?" she asked.

"We don't need one," Deru said, panting slightly. "Varen's Levitation goes down just as well as up."

"Oh," Kirna said.

That sounded well enough, but she had noticed the panting—this fellow Deru was already getting tired, and they weren't even out the window yet.

Well, he had been working magic for hours, which must be tiring, and while Kirna certainly would never have said she was fat, or even stout, she knew she wasn't a frail little twig like some girls—princesses were well-fed. Carrying her might get tiring eventually even for a bigger, stronger man than Deru.

"You're sure you'll be all right?" she asked.

"I'll be fine," he said, and the panting was more obvious this time.

Kirna was hardly in a position to protest, though, so she shut her mouth and watched as they mounted up over the windowsill.

Deru leveled off just a foot or so—no, Kirna corrected herself, perhaps half an inch—above the sill, and walked straight forward, placing each foot solidly on empty air.

The bars were as big as oaks as they passed, great oaks of black iron—and then they were out in the night air, cool and sharp after the hot, stuffy bedchamber. Kirna felt her hair dancing in the breeze, and she squirmed, trying to keep it where it belonged.

"Stop it!" Deru hissed. "You do *not* want me to drop you from here!"

Kirna looked down the side of the tower—and down, and down, and down—and decided that Deru was right. She knew it was only about thirty feet to the ground, at most, but in her shrunken state it looked more like a thousand, and besides, thirty feet was enough to kill someone. She stopped squirming.

Deru marched forward, just as if he were walking on solid stone rather than empty air; then he started descending, step by step, as if he had arrived at another invisible stair.

Kirna, tired of looking down, looked up—and shrieked, "Look out!" She pointed and began struggling desperately.

Deru turned, trying to hold onto his burdens and see what she was talking about. "What is it?" he started to say, but before the words had left his lips he knew what had caused Kirna's panic.

It all happened incredibly fast for Deru; he had been looking down at his feet, watching his descent and staying well clear of tree branches or whatever seeds might be drifting on the wind, since Varen's Levitation would end instantly if either the wizard stopped paying attention, or his booted feet touched solid matter, when Kirna had shouted and begun thrashing. He had turned his attention to the sky and seen nothing but a night-flying bird.

Then it registered that the bird was approaching rapidly, that it was an owl swooping silently toward them.

And then, finally, it registered that this was a *threat*, that in their shrunken state an owl could eat them both.

He instinctly flung up his arms to ward the huge predator off, whereupon Kirna tumbled off his shoulder and plummeted into the darkness beneath.

And at that instant Deru forgot all about Varen's Levitation and dropped the lantern, and he, too, fell into the night. The owl, wings muffled and talons spread, swept harmlessly through the space where the wizard had stood half a second before.

* * * *

Kirna sat up, dazed, trying to remember where she was and what had happened to bring her here. She was sitting on a gigantic leaf, surrounded by a thick tangle of wood; it was dark, though the orange light of the greater moon alleviated the worst of the gloom. To one side she glimpsed an impossibly tall stone tower; everywhere else she saw only forest.

Everything seemed distorted.

Then she remembered why; she was only about two inches tall. That clumsy young wizard had shrunk her, carried her out the window...and then what? Had he carried her off somewhere and abandoned her?

No, he had *dropped* her, when that owl had attacked. She remembered the vast rush of air as she fell, and the utter helpless terror she had felt, and the crunch as she had hit a bush.

The bush must have broken her fall, though, because she was still alive, albeit somewhat bruised and battered.

And she was, she realized, under that same bush, a few feet from Gar's tower.

But where was Deru? Had the owl gotten him?

She scanned the sky overhead as best she could through the tangle of bush, but saw no trace of Deru. She did spot the owl, however, drifting far overhead.

She tried to remember what she knew about owls. Her father, King Tolthar, had insisted she receive a proper education, and while that had mostly meant politics, geography, history, and etiquette, several lessons about her natural surroundings had been included.

She thought the owl up there was a big one, even allowing for her own diminished stature, perhaps even what Tharn the Stablemaster had called a great horned owl, though of course owls didn't actually have horns.

At least, she didn't think they did.

Owls *did* have exceptional eyesight, even for birds, since they preferred to hunt at night. They also had special fringes on their wings that let them fly silently, with none of the audible flapping and rustling of other avians, and they generally gave no cry in flight—hooting was for when they were safely at home, not for when they were out hunting.

That one up there looked very much as if it were hunting.

If it had eaten Deru, she asked herself, wouldn't it be done hunting? She tried to take encouragement from that, to convince herself that this meant Deru was still alive; the possibility that he was simply too small to satisfy so large a bird was too uncomfortable to consider.

For one thing, if the owl had swallowed him she doubted it had managed to remove his pack first, and that was where the antidote to the shrinking spell was. The idea of spending her entire life able to meet chipmunks and large spiders face to face did not appeal to her.

Of course when the owl spat out a pellet of Deru's bones and hair the pack and bottle might still be in it, but that was really too gross to think about. Besides, how would she *find* it?

So she would assume he was still alive, and that he still had that flask in his pack. All she had to do was find him and take a sip, and she would be herself again, and the owl would be no problem at all.

She got to her feet and brushed bits of dry leaf from her gown. She was safe enough here inside this bush, she was sure.

"Deru!" she called, as loudly as she could.

No one answered; she glanced up to see that the owl had wheeled about and was soaring overhead again.

"Deru!" she shouted again.

The owl wavered slightly in its flight, veering toward her.

"Hush!" Deru's voice called back from somewhere a good way off. He sounded strained.

That was an immense relief; she let her breath out in a rush. He was still alive.

She wouldn't have to stay tiny the rest of her life.

"It can't get me here," she called back. "Where *are* you?"

"Over here, in another bush," Deru called back. "Are you *sure* it can't tear its way right through to you?"

Kirna swallowed her reply, suddenly not sure at all. She ducked under one of the larger branches and looked around for better shelter, just in case.

There was a hole in the ground, half-hidden in the darkness; if the owl came for her she could duck in there…

She stopped in mid-thought. *Why* was there a hole in the ground? Presumably something lived in it.

That might be worse than the owl. She had a sudden vision of meeting a snake while still her present size.

"*Do something!*" she shrieked. "Grow back to normal size and get me out of here!"

"I can't!" Deru called back. "I dropped my pack. It's out there in the open somewhere—if I go after it the owl will get me."

"Can't you do *something?*" She was starting to go hoarse from shouting.

"The countercharm needs oak leaves from the very top of a tree ten times the height of a man," Deru called back, his voice sounding weaker. "That's what the tea is made from. Even if these trees are oaks, I can't climb that high when I'm this size!"

"Can't you levitate?"

"Where the owl can see me? Besides, I lost my lantern."

"So what do we *do*?" Her voice cracked on the final word.

"We wait until the owl goes looking for easier prey, and then I fetch my pack from the clearing."

That didn't sound so very difficult—but what if the owl was stubborn? What if Gar noticed her absence and came looking for them? What if whatever lived in that hole came out? Kirna eyed the black opening fearfully.

She didn't really have much choice, though. She looked up.

The owl was still up there. It seemed quite persistent. She wondered if perhaps Gar had put a spell on it so that it would guard the tower.

She waited for what seemed like hours, but which the motion of the greater moon told her was only minutes; then Deru's voice called, "Your Highness?"

"What is it?" she snapped. She was afraid that their conversation was keeping the owl interested, and that it might wake whatever was in that hole.

"I didn't want to worry you, but I think I had better warn you—I hurt myself in the fall. I landed on a thorn. I bandaged it, but I'm still bleeding pretty badly, and I'm not sure I can walk."

"What am *I* supposed to do about it?" Kirna shrieked.

"I thought you should know," Deru called back weakly.

"Idiot!" Kirna shouted. She rammed her fist against a branch of the bush.

This was a nightmare. Everything had gone wrong. When she had followed Gar from Quonmor she had thought she was bound for love and adventure and a life of magic, and now… well, she had gotten some magic, anyway, but she was alone in the dark, dirty and bruised, stuck between a monstrous great bird and a mysterious hole-dweller, with the only one who could help her probably bleeding to death a few feet away.

It wasn't *fair!* She was a princess. These things weren't supposed to happen to her. People were supposed to obey her and protect her, not lock her up or steal her blood and tears or shrink her down to nothing or carry her around like a sack of onions—and *drop* her!

It just wasn't fair at all. The World was not treating her properly.

If she could just find Deru's pack and get the antidote she would be fine, she could go home to her parents and pretend this was all just some grand lark—but that owl was out there, and she didn't know where the pack had fallen. If the owl would just go away…

But it was hungry.

And whatever lived in that hole might be hungry, too. It might come leaping out at her at any moment.

She frowned and looked at the hole. She had had quite enough unpleasant surprises. At least if she knew what lived in there she'd know whether it was dangerous. Whatever it was, it was probably asleep; she could creep down and take a look, then slip back out.

She picked up a big stick—a tiny twig, actually, but to her it was as thick as her arm and somewhat longer than she was tall. Thus armed, she crept across the dead leaves and down the sloping earth into the hole.

She had only gone a few steps when she stopped; ahead of her the hole was utterly black. The moonlight did not reach that far. Going farther suddenly didn't seem like a good idea.

She suddenly wanted to cry. Here she was trying her best to do something useful, something to improve her situation, and it wasn't working. She sniffled.

Then she sniffled again.

There was a smell here, a smell she recognized.

Rabbit.

She suddenly relaxed. This was a rabbit hole! Rabbits wouldn't hurt her, even at this size—they were harmless vegetarians. All she had to worry about was the owl.

That was quite enough, though, if it wouldn't give up and go away. Then a thought struck her.

The owl was staying around because it was hungry, and knew there was prey here. All she had to do was feed it, and it would leave.

She gathered her courage, raised her stick—she was trembling, she realized—and charged forward into the blackness, shouting. "*Hai*, rabbits! Come out, come out! Get out of here!"

There was a sudden stirring in the warm darkness, a rush of air, and she found herself knocked flat against the tunnel wall as something huge and furry pushed past. She flailed wildly with her stick, but whatever it was was gone.

After a moment the racket subsided. She hoped that at least one of the furry idiots had fled out into the open.

She turned and headed out of the tunnel—or started to. At the mouth of the hole she abruptly found herself face to face with a rabbit that had apparently decided its departure had been too hasty.

"Yah!" she shouted, jabbing her stick at the rabbit.

It turned and fled, kicking dirt and bits of leaf at her; she blinked, trying to shield her eyes. Then she pursued.

When she emerged into moonlight she saw that the rabbit was still under the bush; she ran at it, screaming and waving her stick.

The rabbit fled again, hopping out into the clearing…

And then, without a sound, the owl struck.

The rabbit let out a brief squeal, and then bird and prey were both gone, vanished into the night.

For a moment Kirna stared at nothing; the strike had been so fast, so silent, and so sudden that at first she had trouble realizing it had happened.

And when she did, she also realized how close she had come to following the rabbit out of the bush, trying to herd it further. She flung away her stick and let out a strangled gasp.

For a moment she stood there, looking out into the night—first at the clearing, then up at the sky.

The owl was gone. The rabbit was gone. Everything was still.

And Deru's pack was out there somewhere.

It was several minutes before she could work up her nerve to go find it.

She was still searching when Deru staggered out to join her. His face and bare chest were deathly pale, and one leg was wrapped in a bloody bandage made from the tunic he had doffed.

"There," he said, pointing.

She hurried to the spot he indicated, and a moment later she held the precious flask. She turned to Deru.

"Is there any ritual? Anything special we have to do?"

He turned up a palm. "Just drink it. One sip."

She opened the flask and sipped, then handed the rest to Deru—barely in time, as she began growing the instant she swallowed.

The oak-leaf tea had a harsh, slightly nutty taste, but she hardly noticed as she watched the world around her shrink back to normal. The bush she had sheltered beneath, which had seemed as big as a castle, barely reached her waist; the tower wall, while still massive, was no longer the vast World-girdling thing it had been a moment before.

It was also far closer than she had realized.

She looked up at the barred window of her room, and saw that their entire adventure had only taken them a yard or so beyond the bars.

Then Deru, who had been nowhere to be seen, shot up to his old height beside her; she stepped back to avoid catching his elbow in her chest. He staggered.

He looked awful—and, she realized, it was her fault. He had come here to save her. And it had been her own fault she needed saving in the first place.

She hadn't meant for anyone to get hurt. And no one had really meant her any harm, either. She had thrown herself at Gar, and he had taken some advantage of that, but he hadn't tried to hurt her. Even the owl, which would gladly have eaten her, had just been hungry.

Deru had been trying to help, but *he* was the one who got hurt. It wasn't fair.

"Do you have any healing magic in there?" she asked, as he swayed unsteadily on his feet.

"No," he said, "but I've been thinking about it. The Cloak of Ethereality should stop the bleeding and take the weight off my injured leg—I won't weigh anything when I'm ethereal. You start walking; I'll catch up."

"How long will it take?"

"Just a few minutes."

"Then I'll wait," she said.

* * * *

It was still early in the morning of the following day when Princess Kirna, escorted by what appeared to be a crippled wizard's ghost, arrived safely back at Quonmor Keep.

Judging by the expression on her father's face, her arrival was not half as surprising as the first thing she said when shown into the audience chamber.

"I'm sorry, Daddy," she said. "I won't do it again."

He snorted. "We should hope not," he said.

"On the way home Deru explained to me about wizards not being allowed to get involved with royalty," she said. "I need to tell you that Gar didn't really kidnap me; I followed him. I don't want the Wizards' Guild to punish him." In fact, Deru had gone on at some length about how ruthless the Wizards' Guild could be—information that Kirna knew she had heard before, but had never paid the attention it deserved.

Tolthar frowned, clearly puzzled. "We have nothing to do with the Wizards' Guild." He looked at the rather insubstantial presence standing just behind his daughter. "Is this the wizard we hired? He looks…different."

"He's under a spell. He got hurt, and needed to enchant himself until he can get home. You'll still pay him, even though I wasn't kidnapped, won't you?" Deru hadn't said anything about his fee; mentioning it was entirely Kirna's own idea.

Tolthar looked at Deru, who definitely did not look human just now. "Of course," he said, with a rather forced-looking smile. "We wouldn't want to anger a wizard. If we did the Wizards' Guild you mentioned might decide to show us the error of our ways."

Kirna nodded, very seriously. That was exactly what she had been thinking on the way home. Wizardry was powerful stuff. The Wizards' Guild, given a reason, might well swoop down on them.

Just like an owl, she thought.

ABOUT "THE GUARDSWOMAN"

Esther Friesner was putting together an anthology of humorous fantasy about female warriors, preferably in armor—I didn't know yet she was going to call it Chicks in Chainmail. *I had already given some thought to sex roles in Ethshar, and to the difficulties of fitting armor to female bodies, and this story was the result.*

THE GUARDSWOMAN

Dear Mother,

Well, I made it. I'm a soldier in the City Guard of Ethshar of the Sands, in the service of the overlord, Ederd IV.

It wasn't easy!

Getting here wasn't really any trouble. I know you were worried about bandits and...well, and other problems on the highway, but I didn't see any. The people I *did* see didn't bother me at all, unless you count a rude remark one caravan driver made about my size.

He apologized nicely after I stuffed him head-first into a barrel of salted fish.

After that everything went just fine, right up until I reached the city gates. I asked one of the guards about joining up, and *he* made a rude remark, but I couldn't stuff *him* into a fish barrel—for one thing, he had a sword, and I didn't, and he had friends around, and I didn't, and there weren't any barrels right nearby anyway. So I just smiled sweetly and repeated my question, and he sent me to a lieutenant in the north middle tower...

I should explain, I guess. Grandgate is very complicated—it's actually three gates, one after another, with towers on both sides of each gate, so there are six gate-towers, three on the north and three on the south. And each of those towers is connected by a wall to a really *big* tower, and then the city wall itself starts on the other side of each of the *big* towers, which are the North Barracks and the South Barracks. Everything right along the highway, out to the width of the outer gate, which is the widest one, is part of Grandgate Market, and everyone just walks right through if they want to and if the guards don't decide they shouldn't. Everything between the inner towers and the barracks towers, though, is sort of private territory for us guards—that's where we train, and march, and so on.

Anyway, the gateman sent me to a lieutenant in the north middle tower, and *he* sent me to Captain Dabran in the North Barracks, and he sent me back to another lieutenant, Lieutenant Gerath, in the north outer tower, to see whether I could qualify.

I had to do all kinds of things to show I was strong and fast enough—most women aren't, after all, so I guess it was fair. I had a foot-race with a man named Lador, and then after I beat him I had to catch him and throw him over a fence-rail, and then I had to pick up this fellow named Talden who's just about the fattest man you ever saw, Mother, I mean he's even fatter than Parl the Smith, and throw *him* over the fence-rail. I tried to find nice soft mud for them to land in, but I'm not sure if they appreciated it. The lieutenant did, though.

And then I had to climb a rope to the top of the tower, and throw a spear, and on and on.

The worst part was the swordsmanship test. Mother, no one in the village knows how to use a sword properly, not the way these people do! Lieutenant Gerath says I'll need to really work on using a sword. That prompted some rude remarks from the other soldiers about women knowing what to do with swords, only they didn't mean *sword* swords, of course, but they all shut up when I glared at them and then looked meaningfully at the fence rail and the mud.

By the time I finished all the tests, though, a whole crowd had gathered to watch, and they were laughing and cheering—I never *saw* so many people! There were more people there than there are in our entire village!

And I was exhausted, too—but Lieutenant Gerath was really impressed, and he vouched for me to Captain Dabran, and here I am! I'm a soldier! They've given me my yellow tunic and everything.

I don't have a red skirt yet, though—all they had on hand were kilts, and of course I want to wear something decent, not walk around with my legs bare. It must be cold in the winter, going around like that.

Anyway, they didn't have any proper skirts; they're going to give me the fabric and let me make my own. And they didn't have any breastplates that fit—naturally, one that was meant for a man isn't going to fit *me*. I'm not shaped like that. The armorer is working on making me one.

I asked why they didn't have any for women, and everyone kind of looked embarrassed, so I kept asking, and...

Well, Mother, you know we've always heard that the City Guard is open to anyone over sixteen who can handle the job, man or woman, and everyone here swears that's true, so I asked how many women there are in the Guard right now, and everyone got even *more* embarrassed, but finally Captain Dabran answered me.

One.

Me.

There have been others in the past, though not for several years, and they wouldn't mind more in the future, but right now, there's just me.

I guess it's a great honor, but I wonder whether it might get a bit *lonely*. It's going to be hard to fit in.

I mean, right now, I'm writing this while sitting alone in the North Barracks. I have my own room here, since I'm the only woman in the Guard, but even if I didn't, I'd be alone. Everyone else who's off duty went out. I asked where they were going, you know, hinting that I'd like to come along, but when I found out where they were going I decided I'd stay here and write this letter.

They're going down to the part of the city called Soldiertown, where all the tradespeople who supply the Guard are. I've been down there—to Tavern Street, and Sword Street, and Armorer Street, and Gambler Street.

Except tonight, they're all going to Whore Street.

Somehow I figured it would be better if I didn't go along.

Well, I guess that's about everything I had to say. I'm a soldier now, and I'm fine, and I hope everything's fine back home. Say hello to Thira and Kara for me.

Your loving daughter,

Shennar

* * * *

Dear Mother,

I'm sorry I haven't written sooner, but I've been pretty busy. The work isn't all that hard, but we don't get much time off.

Well, I *could* have written sooner, but…

Well, anyway, I'm writing *now.*

Everything's fine here. I got my uniform completed—the armorer had a lot of trouble with the breastplate, but he got it right eventually. Or almost right; it's still a bit snug.

I've been here for two months now, and mostly it's been fine. I don't mind standing guard at the gate, or walking the top of the wall, or patrolling the market, and so far I haven't had to arrest anyone or break up any fights. Not any *real* fights, anyway—nothing where picking someone up and throwing him away didn't solve the problem.

And my time off-duty has been all right; most of the men treat me well, though they're a lot rougher than I'm used to. I don't mind that; I can be rough right back without worrying about hurting anyone.

But I'm not sure I'm really fitting in. I mean, everyone's nice to me, and they all say they like having me here, but I don't really feel like I'm part of the company yet, if you know what I mean. I'm still the new kid.

And it doesn't help any that once every sixnight, all the men in my barracks hall go down to Whore Street, and the whole place is empty, and I can't go along.

The first time they did that I just sat here and wrote to you, and then tidied up the place, and kept busy like that, but the second time I was determined to *do* something.

So I tried going downstairs to one of the other barracks halls—I'm on the fourth floor of the North Barracks—but I didn't know anybody there, and they were all busy with their regular off-duty stuff. The only way I could see to get in on anything would be to join the game of three-bone going on in the corner, and I'm not very good at dice, so I didn't.

Then I tried going into the city, but I went in uniform, and the minute I walked into a tavern everyone shut up and stared at me. That wasn't very comfortable.

I thought maybe they'd get over it, so I bought an ale and sat down at an empty table and waited for someone to come over and join me, but no one did.

It wasn't much fun.

When I finished my ale I came back here and sat around being utterly miserable. I felt completely left out; it was as bad as when the village kids wouldn't play with me because I was so big and strong. I didn't exactly cry myself to sleep, but I sniffled a little.

The next day all my barracksmates were back, laughing and joking and feeling good. I made some remarks, and Kelder Arl's son said, "Well, Shennar, at some of the houses there are boys for rent, too." And everyone laughed.

I didn't think it was very funny, myself. And I certainly didn't take it seriously. I don't understand why the men all go to the brothels, anyway—they're mostly decent people, and could find women elsewhere. Some of them *have* women elsewhere, but they go to Whore Street anyway.

Men are strange.

But it did get me thinking that what I needed was some nice young man I could visit every sixnight. It wouldn't really do to bed with one of my fellow soldiers; I wouldn't feel right about that. Besides, most of them aren't *that* nice. I wanted a civilian.

So I started looking for one. I wore my civilian clothes and went to the most respectable inns and shops and tried to act like a lady.

Honestly, Mother, you'd think that in a city this size, it wouldn't be hard to find a good man, but I certainly didn't manage it. For sixnight after sixnight I looked, and I found plenty of drunkards and foul-smelling wretches, and big stupid oxen, and men who might have been all right if they weren't so small I was afraid that I'd break them in half if I ever hugged them.

And, well, I gave up, and here I am writing this letter while the men are at the brothels again.

What *is* it that makes them so eager to spend all their money there?

Mother, you know what I'm going to do? I'm going to seal this up for the messenger, and then I'm going to go down to Whore Street and *ask* someone. Not one of my barracksmates, but someone who works there. I'll just *ask* why the men all go there every sixnight.

Maybe if I can figure *that* out, it'll give me some idea what I should do!

Love,

Shennar

* * * *

Dear Mother,

I met the most wonderful man! And you'll never guess where.

I'd gone down to Whore Street, the way I told you I was planning to, and at first I just walked up and down the street—it's only seven blocks long—just looking at the brothels and listening to the people. But after awhile that wasn't getting me anywhere, so I got up my nerve and went up to one of the doors and knocked.

This woman who wasn't wearing anything but a chiffon skirt and a feather in her hair answered, and took one look at me, and said, "I'm sorry, but you must have the wrong place." And she tried to shut the door.

Well, I wasn't going to give up that easily; I was afraid that I'd never be able to get up the nerve to try again if I once backed down. So I put my foot in the door and pushed back.

I tried to tell her I just wanted to talk to someone, but she wasn't listening; instead she was calling, "Tabar! Tabar, quick!"

I pushed in through the door and I tried to catch her by the arm, since she wasn't wearing any tunic I could grab, but I couldn't get a solid hold, and then this voice deep as distant thunder said, "Is there a problem?"

And I looked up—really *up*, Mother! And there was this face looking down at me with the most spectacular mustache and big dark eyes.

"She wouldn't let me in," I said, and I let the woman go. She ran off and left me face to face with this *huge* man—we'd have been nose to nose if he hadn't been so tall.

"We don't accept women as customers here," he said. "You could try Beautiful Phera's Place, two doors down."

"I'm not a customer," I told him.

"If you have a complaint you can tell *me*," he said. "Though I don't promise we'll do anything about it."

"It's not a complaint, exactly," I said, "but I'd like to talk to you."

He nodded, and led the way to a little room off to one side.

And while we were walking there I got a good look at two things.

One was the front room. It was amazing. Silk and velvet everywhere, and beads, and colored glass, all in reds and pinks and yellows.

And the other was the man I was talking to. Mother, he was taller than Father! And *much* broader. I'd never seen anyone *close* to that size before! He had lovely long black hair, and these long fingers, and that *wonderful* mustache. He was wearing a black velvet tunic worked with gold, and a black kilt, and he moved like a giant *cat*, Mother, it was just gorgeous.

Anyway, we went into this little room, which was very small, and pretty ordinary, with a little table and a couple of chairs, and we sat down, and he looked at me, didn't say anything.

I couldn't help asking, "Why aren't you in the *Guard*?"

He smiled at me. "You must be new around here," he said. "Think about it. A guardsman—or guardswoman—has to be big and strong enough to stop a fight, preferably before it starts. You've probably seen a guardsman stop trouble just by standing up and frowning, or by walking in the door and shouting—guards hardly ever have to draw their swords."

"I've done it myself," I admitted.

"Well," he said, "this is Soldiertown. Most of the customers here are guardsmen. If *they* start trouble, Rudhira wants to have someone around who can stop guardsmen the way guardsmen stop ordinary tavern brawls. So she hired me."

He wasn't bragging, Mother. He turned up a palm, you know what I mean. He was just stating a fact.

"But wouldn't you rather be in the Guard?" I asked.

He looked at me as if I had gone mad, then laughed.

"Rudhira pays better," he said. "And there are extras."

"Oh," I said, and then I realized what the extras probably were, and I blushed and said, "Oh," again.

"Some houses use magicians to handle trouble," he said conversationally. "After all, we all need to have the magicians in sometimes to make sure nobody catches anything, and some of the girls want magic to be sure they don't get pregnant, so why not use them to keep things peaceful? But if a customer's drunk enough he might not notice a magician right away, and magic takes time, and can go wrong—and besides, I cost more than a guardsman, but not as much as a wizard! So Rudhira keeps my brother and me around, and we make sure everything stays quiet and friendly and no one gets rough." He leaned back, and asked, "So why are you here?"

So I explained about how all my barracksmates would disappear every sixnight, and how tired I was of being left with nothing to do, and I asked why they all came *here*, instead of finding themselves women...I mean, finding women who aren't professionals.

"Oh, it's all part of showing off to each other that they're real men," Tabar said. "They all come here because they can do it *together*, and show how loyal they all are to each other. The more stuff they do together, the more they trust each other when there's trouble."

I had to think about that for awhile, but eventually I decided he was right. If one of the men went off with his own woman, he wouldn't be as much a part of the company.

But of course, that meant that *I* wasn't as much a part of the company.

I'd sort of noticed that, as I guess I told you, but I thought it was just because I was new, and not from the city, and of course partly because I was the only woman. I tried to fit in, and I did everything that everyone else did back at the barracks, all the jokes and games and arm-wrestling and so on, and mostly it was okay, but I could feel that I wasn't *really* accepted yet, and I thought it was just going to be a matter of time—but when Tabar explained that I realized that it wasn't just that. The expeditions down to Whore Street were part of fitting in, and I wasn't doing it.

I *couldn't*, unless I wanted to go to someplace like Beautiful Phera's, which I didn't, and besides, none of my company went to places like that—they all liked women, or at least pretended to when they went to Whore Street, and the specialty places charged extra.

Even before I asked Tabar about it, I knew that didn't really make any difference that I couldn't.

Anyway, I got talking to Tabar about it all, and we talked and talked, and by the time I headed back to the barracks it was just about midnight.

And the next sixnight, when the men were getting ready to go, I had an idea. I said, "Hey, wait for me!" and I went along with them.

Some of them were kind of nervous about it; I could see that in the way they looked at me, and they weren't as noisy as usual. One man—you don't know him, but his name's Kelder Arl's son—asked where I thought I was going, and I said, "Rudhira's." And everyone laughed.

"You like women?" someone asked, and someone else said, "Or are you trying to pick up a few extra silvers?" And I didn't get mad or anything, I just laughed and said no.

I didn't get mad because I knew Tabar would be there.

As soon as we set foot in the door I called, "Tabar!" And there he was, and he stopped dead in his tracks when he saw me, and this big grin spread all over his face.

"Shennar," he said, "what are *you* doing here?"

"The boys and I are just here for our regular fun," I said, and everyone laughed, and we had a fine time. I talked to some of the girls, and joked with the men, and then when the men went upstairs Tabar and I went back to his room…

He's wonderful, Mother. If you ever come down to visit you'll have to meet him.

Love,
Shennar

* * * *

Dear Mother,

What's wrong with a whorehouse bouncer? It's honest work.

Mother, I'm not a delicate little flower. I'm a hundred and eighty pounds of bone and muscle. And Tabar is two hundred and fifty pounds of bone and muscle. I like him.

And seeing him has really helped. I'm fitting in better than ever. I love my job, Mother, and going to Whore Street every sixnight is helping me with it.

Besides, I like Tabar a *lot*, Mother. And it's not as if it costs me anything, the way it does everyone else. Tabar and I joke sometimes about which of us should be charging.

The only thing is…

Well, it looks as if Tabar and I will be married, at least for awhile. We hadn't really planned on it, but it's happened. The lieutenant says I can get leave when I need it, and I've been saving up what the men use as brothel money so I won't starve while I'm on leave, but I'm not sure how it's going to go over with the rest of the company having a baby around here.

I think they'll get used to it. But it's driving the armorer crazy enlarging my breastplate every sixnight or so!

Love,

Shennar

ABOUT "WEAVING SPELLS"

Readers seem to be fascinated by the Transporting Tapestries I introduced in With A Single Spell, *so it seemed reasonable to write a story about how they're made, and an anthology invitation came along at just the right time—an anthology Marion Zimmer Bradley was editing that had no specific theme beyond fantasy. So I wrote this.*

WEAVING SPELLS

Kirinna had been staring out the farmhouse window at the steady rain for several minutes, worrying about Dogal, when she got up so suddenly that her chair fell backward and crashed on the floor. Her mother jumped at the sudden sound, dropping a stitch. The older woman looked up.

"I'm going after him," Kirinna announced.

"Oh, I don't—" her mother began, lowering her knitting.

"You are not," her father announced from the doorway; he had risen at the sound of the toppling chair and come to see what had caused the commotion.

"Father, Dogal and I are supposed to be *married* tomorrow!" Kirinna said, turning. "He should have been back home days ago, and he isn't! What are you going to do tomorrow, keep the whole village standing around while we wait for him?"

"If he's not here, then the wedding will be postponed," her father said. "You are *not* going to go running off in the rain looking for him—what if he comes home while you're away, and *you're* the one who misses the wedding?"

"Is it any worse that way? It's still early. I'll be back tonight, I promise."

"That's what Dogal said," Kirinna's mother said worriedly.

"Which is why you aren't going *anywhere*, girl," her father said, pointing a hand at Kirinna. "Now, you pick up that chair and settle down to your work." He gestured at the bowl of peas Kirinna had been shelling before her worries got the better of her.

Kirinna stared at him for a minute, then sighed; all the fight seemed to go out of her.

"Yes, Father," she said. She stooped and reached for the chair.

Her father watched for a moment, then turned to resume his own efforts in the back room, polishing the ornamental brass for tomorrow's planned celebration.

Kirinna fiddled with the chair, brushed at her skirt, adjusted the bowl—and then, when she was sure both her parents had settled to their work, she ran lightly across the room to the hearth, where she reached up and snatched her great-grandfather's sword down from its place on the mantle.

"What are you…?" her mother began, but before the sentence was finished Kirinna was out the door and running through the warm spring rain, the sheathed sword clutched in one hand, her house-slippers splashing noisily through the puddles as she dashed through the village toward the coast road.

A moment later her father was standing in the doorway, shouting after her, but she ignored him and ran on.

She didn't need anyone's permission, she told herself. She was a grown woman, past her eighteenth birthday and about to wed, and the man she loved needed her. It wasn't as if she intended to run off blindly into the wilderness; she knew where Dogal had gone, knew exactly what he had planned the day he disappeared, a sixnight earlier.

A strange stone the size of a man's head had fallen from the sky during the winter and landed in Dogal's back pasture, melting a great circle of snow and plowing a hole in the earth beneath, and everyone knew that such stones were rare and of great value to magicians. When the spring planting was done and the wedding preparations in hand Dogal had set out three leagues down the coast, to sell the sky-stone to the famous wizard Alladia, said to be one of the richest and most powerful in all the western lands.

He had teased Kirinna about how she might spend the money once they were married, and she had laughed and given him a shove on his way.

And he hadn't come back.

Some of the village children had teased her when Dogal didn't return, far less kindly than had her betrothed, saying he had run off with someone else—that he hadn't gone to Alladia at all, but to some rival's house, rather than stay to wed crazy, short-tempered Kirinna.

Kirinna knew better than that. Dogal loved her.

Other villagers had suggested that perhaps Dogal had angered Alladia somehow, and been turned into a mouse or a frog, or simply been slain. *That* possibility was far too real, though she couldn't imagine how poor sweet Dogal could have annoyed the wizard that much. She had been telling herself for two or three days now that Alladia couldn't be so cruel.

But then there was a third suggestion—that Alladia had decided to keep handsome young Dogal for herself, and had ensorcelled him. Kirinna found that theory all too easy to believe; certainly *she* had wanted Dogal from the first moment she had laid eyes on him, and Alladia was said to be young for a wizard, certainly young enough to still appreciate the company of men.

If the wizard thought Kirinna was going to give her man up without a fight, though, she was very wrong indeed—and that was why Kirinna had snatched her great-grandfather's sword. It was said that during the Great War old Kinner had once killed a Northern sorcerer with this very blade; Kirinna hoped she could do as well with it against an Ethsharitic wizard.

Of course, Kinner had been a trained soldier, with years of experience and all the magical protection General Gor's wizards could provide, while Kirinna had never used a sword in her life—but she tried not to think of that as she marched down the road.

She had gone less than half a league when she paused to mount the scabbarded weapon properly on her belt; carrying it in her hand was tiresome and unnecessary. She settled the sheath in place and drew the sword, just to test it.

She was startled by how fine and light the blade was, how the weight of the sword was so perfectly balanced that her hand seemed to almost move of its own volition as she took a few practice swings.

She remembered to wipe it dry before sheathing it again; then she jogged onward down the road, trotting to make up the time she had spent trying the sword.

The rain stopped when she had gone a little more than a league from her parents' home, and the skies were clearing by the time she finally came in sight of the wizard's home.

She had left the ill-kept road for the rocky beach half a league back, scrambling across grassy dunes and wave-polished rocks. Alladia's house was perched on a bluff overlooking the ocean; as Kirinna watched the sun broke through the clouds and painted a line of gold along the water that seemed to burst at the end into a shower of sparks that were the reflections in Alladia's dozens of windows.

It was the biggest house Kirinna had ever seen; she wondered whether even the overlord's Fortress in Ethshar of the Rocks could be larger. Three stories high, not counting a tower at one end that rose another two levels, and easily a hundred feet from end to end—Kirinna had never imagined anything so grand.

The main entrance was on the other side, she knew—that was one reason she had come along the beach. She had no intention of walking up to the wizard's front door and politely asking if anyone had seen a young man named Dogal; she planned to get inside that house and see for herself. She began clambering up the bluff.

At the top she heaved herself up over the final outcropping of rock and found herself staring in a window, her face just inches from the glass.

She was looking into a wizard's house, and she half-expected to see all manner of monstrosities, but instead she saw an ordinary room—paved in gray stone, as if the entire floor were hearth, but otherwise unremarkable. An oaken table stood against one wall, with a pair of candlesticks and a bowl of flowers arranged on it and chairs at either end; a rag rug covered perhaps half the stone floor. There were no cauldrons, no skulls, no strange creatures scurrying about.

She hesitated, considering whether to find a door or simply smash her way in, and compromised by drawing her belt-knife and digging into the leading between windowpanes. A few minutes' work was enough to loosen one square of glass, and she pried at one edge, trying to pop it free of its mangled frame.

The sheet of glass snapped, and shards tumbled at her feet; she froze, listening and peering into the house, fearing someone had heard the noise.

Apparently no one had; the only sounds she heard were the waves breaking beneath her and the wind in the eaves.

She reached into the hole she had made, unlatched the window, and swung it open; then she climbed carefully into the house.

The room was bigger and finer and cleaner than most she had seen, but looked no more outlandish from inside than it had through the glass—she had thought there might be some sort of illusion at work, altering the room's appearance when seen from outside, but if so it worked inside, too. She crept carefully out to the center of the room and stood on the rag rug, looking around.

Doorways opened into three other rooms—one appeared to be a dining hall, another a storeroom stacked with dusty wooden boxes, and the third she couldn't identify. None were visibly inhabited.

She transferred her belt-knife to her left hand and drew her great-grandfather's sword. There should be guards, she thought—either hired men, or supernatural beings of some sort, or at least spells. In the family stories of the Great War wizards were all part of the Ethsharitic military, and always had soldiers around, as well as their magic.

Kirinna saw no soldiers here—and for that matter, no magic. Breaking in the window might have triggered some sort of magical warning somewhere, but she no sign of anything out of the ordinary.

She also saw no sign of the wizard Alladia, or of Dogal. All she saw was a big, comfortable house.

She crept to the nearest doorway and peered through, half-expecting a guard to jump out and knock the sword from her hand; she clutched the hilt so tightly her knuckles ached.

All she saw was a dining hall, with a big bare table and half a dozen chairs and a magnificent china cabinet.

Something thumped, and she froze; it sounded again, and she realized it was coming from the cabinet.

Was someone in there? Could Dogal have been stuffed in there, somehow? She moved nervously across the room, dashing a few steps and then pausing to look in all directions, until she reached the cabinet and opened one of the brightly-painted doors.

A cream-colored ceramic teapot was strolling up and down the shelf on stubby red porcelain legs, bumping against pots and platters.

"Dogal?" she asked, wondering if her beloved had somehow been transformed into crockery.

The teapot ignored her and ambled on until it tripped over a salt-cellar and bumped its spout on the side of the cabinet; then it stopped, and somehow managed to look disgruntled as it righted itself and settled down on the shelf.

There was magic here, certainly, but nothing she could connect with Dogal; Kirinna closed the cabinet and moved on.

She made her way through room after room, from study to kitchen to privy, without being challenged or impeded and without finding anything else out of the ordinary except general displays of wealth and a remarkable number of storerooms. She began to fear that the house was deserted, that Alladia had fled somewhere with Dogal.

Finally, she heard footsteps overhead—the house was not deserted! Someone *was* here! She hurried to the nearer of the two staircases she had discovered and crept up the steps, sword still ready in her hand.

At the top of the stairs she found herself at one end of a hallway; she could smell incense and other, less-identifiable scents, and could hear an unfamiliar low rattling and thumping. Warily, she made her way down the hall, following the sounds and odors.

She came at last to an open door that was definitely the source; she crept up beside the doorframe and turned to peer in.

A woman was seated with her back to the door, working at a sort of loom—but not a loom quite like any Kirinna had ever seen before, as it had odd angles built into it, and extra structures projecting here and there. The whole construction was wrapped in a thick haze of incense, but she could see levers, weights, and pulleys in peculiar arrangements. Although a high window let daylight into the room three tall candles stood atop the frame, burning brightly amid mounds of melted wax, while the fabric being woven glittered strangely, as if points of light were being worked directly into the pattern.

Kirinna had sometimes heard people speak of magicians weaving spells, but she had always assumed it to be a metaphor, a description based on the intricate gestures wizards used in their conjuring; now she saw that perhaps it could be meant literally. This woman was surely Alladia, working some dire magic on her wood-and-rope framework.

The woman seemed oblivious to everything but her work, and Kirinna stepped around the doorjamb, intending to march in and demand an explanation at swordpoint of Dogal's disappearance.

Instead she collided with someone, or something, that had been out of her line of sight and had turned to come through the door at the same moment she did. She had a glimpse of a bearded face and a thick homespun tunic, and then someone was grabbing her wrists, shouting, "*Hai!* Out! Stay out!"

Here was the guard she had been expecting. She tore her hands free and tried to raise her sword to strike, but the flat of the blade slapped into the underside of the man's arm and was harmlessly deflected; then his knee came up and caught her painfully in the belly, and she staggered back into the hallway. That dragged her sword's edge across the man's raised thigh, and he yelped in pain and stepped back.

Kirinna swept disarrayed hair from her face with her left hand, raised the sword with her right—then stopped.

The bearded man was Dogal. He was bent over, clutching his leg, where blood was seeping from a slash in his breeches; his hair and beard were somewhat longer than Kirinna remembered, and far more unkempt, but it was unmistakably Dogal.

"Augh!" Kirinna said. "She's ensorcelled you!" She lowered the sword—then raised it again.

Dogal looked up from his wound, and got his first clear look at her face.

"Kirinna?" He stared, his bleeding leg forgotten. "What are *you* doing here?"

At least he remembered who she was, despite being in the wizard's thrall. "I came to get you," she said. "We're to be married tomorrow—has her spell made you forget?"

"What spell? Where did you get a *sword?*"

Kirinna hesitated. Dogal didn't *sound* enchanted—just confused. And the wizard herself was still busily at work at the loom, ignoring the discussion just a few feet away.

"It was my great-grandfather's," she said. "From the war."

Dogal looked down at his ruined breeches. The blood had stopped; the cut obviously wasn't very deep. "It's still sharp," he said.

"My father cleans it every year during Festival," Kirinna said. She felt foolish explaining such mundane details while facing her beloved at swordpoint in a wizard's workshop, surrounded by incense and magic, but she could not think what *else* she should say.

"I hadn't forgotten the wedding," Dogal said. "I would have been there, really—at least, I hope so. We should be finished tonight if nothing goes wrong."

Kirinna looked at the wizard. "Finished with *what?*" she asked. "Is she tired of you already?"

At that the wizard glanced briefly over her shoulder at Kirinna before returning to her work; the face Kirinna glimpsed was rather ordinary, round and soft, with a large nose and wide mouth.

"*Tired* of me?" Dogal looked utterly baffled. "No, the tapestry will be finished, that's all."

Kirinna looked from Dogal to the wizard and back; then she lowered the sword warily.

"What's going on?" she said. "Why didn't you come home?"

She was not necessarily convinced yet that Dogal wasn't under a spell, but he seemed so normal, so much himself, that she was willing to consider it unproven either way, and the wizard's complete failure to intervene had her fairly certain that she did not know what was happening.

Dogal sighed. "Can we go somewhere else to talk?" he asked. "Somewhere I can sit down and get away from the smell of incense?"

"She'll allow it?" Kirinna asked, pointing the sword at the wizard.

"Of course she will; I just finished my turn at the loom."

"Go on," the wizard called, the first words Kirinna had heard her speak. "Go away and stop distracting me."

Now completely defeated by awareness of her own ignorance, Kirinna sheathed her blades. "Come on, then," she said.

A moment later Dogal and Kirinna were seated in one of the downstairs rooms, and Dogal began his explanation.

"When I came here to sell Alladia the sky-stone I found the front door standing open, so I came in, calling out," he said. "She heard me and replied, and I followed her voice up the stairs to that workroom, where she was laboring at the loom. She looked half-dead from exhaustion, spending as much time repairing her own fumble-fingered mistakes as weaving new cloth, but she couldn't stop without losing the entire spell. She'd been working on it for sixnights, with the help of her apprentice, but a few days before he had gotten scared and run off—he'd even left the door standing open, the inconsiderate brat—and she had gone on without him, trying to finish it by herself. She was ready to collapse."

Kirinna, who knew Dogal well, suddenly understood. "So you stayed to help."

Dogal smiled. "Yes, of course. I brought her food and water, and she showed me what had to be done so I could work on it while she slept, and since then we've taken turns."

"Wasn't there some way you could have let us know?"

He turned up a palm. "How? I didn't dare leave for long enough to go home and come back—besides, I knew that our families might not let me return here. And she can't work any other spells until this one is completed—that's part of the magic—so she couldn't send a message."

"Would it really have been so terrible if she couldn't finish the spell?" Kirinna asked wistfully. "We were so *worried* about you!"

"It might have been. You must have heard the stories about spells gone wrong."

Kirinna couldn't argue with that; she had, indeed, heard stories about catastrophes caused by interrupted wizardry. The Tower of Flame, somewhere in the southern Small Kingdoms, was said to still be burning after more than three hundred years, and that had been simply a spell meant to light a campfire in the rain—a spell that had been interrupted by a sneeze.

"What *is* the spell she's working on?"

"It's called a Transporting Tapestry," Dogal explained. "When it's finished, touching it will instantly transport one to the place pictured." He added, "They're extremely valuable, even by the standards of wizards."

"I can see why," Kirinna admitted.

"She's promised to pay me well for assisting her, as well as for the stone," Dogal said. "Once it's done."

"So you're staying until then." It wasn't really a question; Kirinna knew how stubborn Dogal could be.

"Yes."

"Then I'll stay, too," Kirinna declared. She could be stubborn, too. "And I can help with the weaving."

Dogal frowned. "That's not necessary," he said.

"Yes, it is," Kirinna said. "I'm not leaving *my* man alone here with a grateful woman!"

Kirinna saw from Dogal's expression that he knew better than to argue with her, but he said, "What if it takes longer than we thought? Your parents will worry."

"And we'll have to put the wedding off for a few days," Kirinna agreed.

"Your parents *will* worry," Dogal said. "In fact, they may come here after us."

"We'll send them a message," Kirinna declared.

"Kirinna, if you go home to tell them, it's hardly worth coming back—"

"I'm not going *anywhere*," Kirinna declared.

"Well, I'm not, either, until the spell is done. And I already told you Alladia can't work any other spells. So how do you propose to send a message?"

Kirinna sighed. "Dogal, I love you, but sometimes you just aren't as clever as you might be. Didn't you explore this house while you were here?"

He simply stared at her blankly. It wasn't until she led him into the dining hall and opened the cabinet that he finally understood.

Kirinna's parents had just sat down to a late, lonely, and worried supper that night when a thumping brought her mother to the front door. She opened the door, and a cream-colored teapot promptly walked in on stubby red legs, a roll of parchment stuck in its spout.

The wedding was postponed a twelvenight, but at last Kirinna and Dogal stood happily together in the village square, speaking the ceremonial oaths that would bind them as husband and wife.

They were dressed rather more elaborately than Kirinna had expected, due to a sudden increase in their personal wealth, and the rather modest wedding supper that had originally been planned had become a great feast. Alladia had paid Dogal a full tenth of the Tapestry's value—more money than the village had ever before seen in one place.

And Alladia herself watched the vows; Kirinna smiled so broadly at the sight of her that she had trouble pronouncing the words of her promises to Dogal. The wizard stood nearby, slightly apart from the crowd—the other villagers all stayed at least a few feet away from her, out of respect or fear.

When the ritual was complete and she had kissed Dogal properly Kirinna quickly gave her parents and Dogal's mother and sisters the traditional embraces, signifying that the marriage was accepted by all concerned, then hurried over to hug Alladia.

"Thank you for coming!" she said.

"Thank you for having me, and congratulations to you both," Alladia replied. She lifted a pack that lay by her ankle and opened it, then pulled out a wrapped bundle. "For you."

Kirinna blinked in surprise. "You already paid us more than enough," she said.

"I paid Dogal," Alladia corrected her. "This is for you."

The villagers had gathered around to see what the wizard had brought. Wondering, Kirinna opened the bundle and found a fine decanter of glittering colored glass. "It's beautiful!" she exclaimed.

"It isn't animated, like my teapot," Alladia said, "but I thought you'd like it. It's from Shan on the Desert—I bought it there myself."

"But Shan on the Desert is more than a hundred leagues from here!" one of the neighbors exclaimed.

Kirinna smiled. She knew what scene was depicted on the tapestry she and Dogal had helped create.

"She knows a shorter route," Kirinna said.

ABOUT "THE GOD IN RED"

We've been making our own Christmas/Yule/solstice/Chanukah/ whatever cards for decades. Usually they're pretty much your standard card, with a captioned picture on the front and a holiday greeting or punchline inside. Sometimes the art was commissioned, sometimes my daughter Kiri drew it, sometimes it was kludged together somehow. The idea was usually the result of a family conference, occasionally one person's brainstorm. Some of them have been pretty good, if I do say so myself, and I keep meaning to put a gallery of them up on the web, but I always felt as if, as a writer, I should be writing something more substantial than a mere card. I mean, John M. Ford wrote "Winter Solstice, Camelot Station" as a Christmas card, and I've gotten stories in cards, or as cards, from various other writers, ranging from short-shorts to an entire novel, so I felt I should be doing something along those lines. Coming up with a good idea for a Christmas story isn't that easy, though, and so far I've only done it once. This was the result.

And yes, this is an official Ethshar story. It's in continuity, as they say in comics. It is not necessarily, however, the real Santa Claus who appears.

THE GOD IN RED

Darrend the apprentice theurgist paused in his invocation long enough to take a deep breath, then moved his fingers in the odd, jerky rhythm his mistress, Alir of Priest Street, had taught him. He continued, "*Awir thigo lan takloz...*"

He hesitated. That didn't sound right. Alir wasn't stopping him, though, and he could still feel the peculiar pressure of gathering magic. The spell to summon the goddess Piskor the Generous was almost complete. "*Takloz wesfir yu!* Your generosity is needed!" he finished.

And then he sensed a *presence* in the room, and he closed his eyes quickly lest he be dazzled by Piskor's radiance, but there was no burst of light, no increase in pressure, none of the feeling of being somehow both in the World and out of it simultaneously that ordinarily accompanied the presence of a deity.

He opened his eyes, unsure whether he would see the empty room, or the majestic beauty of the goddess Piskor.

Then he blinked once, and stared. He glanced up at his mistress, but she, too, was staring.

Someone had appeared, but he was definitely not Piskor. He didn't look like a god at all, and Darrend remembered that sometimes when an invocation went wrong it would summon a demon instead, but this didn't look like a demon, either. It looked like a fat old man in a bright red coat trimmed with white fur, his beard and hair long and equally white, his mouth turned up in a broad smile, his eyes twinkling. He had scuffed black boots on his feet, and a large brown sack slung over one shoulder.

And he looked at least as surprised to be there as Darrend was at seeing him.

"The word is *takkoz*," Alir said, without taking her eyes off this apparition. "Not *takloz*, just *takkoz*."

"Oh," Darrend said. "So I didn't summon Piskor?"

"No."

"Who did I summon instead, then?"

"I have no idea," Alir said. Then she addressed the stranger. "Do you speak Ethsharitic?"

"I speak everything," he said, in a deep, rich, cheerful voice. "It's part of the job."

Alir and Darrend exchanged glances.

"Who are you?" Alir asked.

"You don't recognize me?" His merry eyes widened still further in surprise.

"Should we?"

The red-clad figure set down his bag and laughed heartily at that. "Pardon me," he said. "I'm accustomed to being recognized everywhere I go, and it's a good lesson to me to be reminded there are places I *don't* go." He chuckled, and set his sack on the floor. "If you'll forgive me for asking, where *am* I?"

"You're in my workroom on Priest Street, in the Wizards' Quarter of Ethshar of the Spices."

The stranger nodded thoughtfully. "And where is Ethshar of the Spices? Asia, perhaps?"

Again, Darrend and Alir looked at one another before Alir replied, "It's the largest city in the Hegemony of the Three Ethshars."

"And that is . . . where?"

Baffled, Alir said, "Between the ocean and the mountains, from Tintallion to the Small Kingdoms."

"My dear, you have yet to say a name I recognize, and I had thought I knew *everywhere*."

"And you have yet to tell us who you are," Alir pointed out.

"So I haven't! Well, I have many names, but the most popular is Santa Claus."

"*Takloz!*" Darrend exclaimed.

"That would explain how we got you instead of Piskor," Alir acknowledged. "Are you a god?"

"My heavens, no!" the stranger said, with another laugh.

"A demon?" Darrend asked.

"Certainly not!"

"Then what *are* you?" Alir demanded.

"Oh, now, you'd think that would be easy to answer, wouldn't you? But I'm afraid it's not. I'm a myth, a saint, an elf, a spirit, a jolly old man—it all depends on who you ask."

"A spirit, you said. Spirit of what?"

"Oh, of giving, of kindness and generosity, of..." He paused, looking surprised. "How curious; your language doesn't seem to have a word for '*Christmas,*' or even one that comes close."

"'*Christmas?*'"

"A holiday in winter. There's quite a story that goes with it, if you're interested—many stories, really."

"I don't think we're interested. Not just now."

"What a pity!"

"A spirit of generosity named Santakloz." Alir frowned. "Well, I can see how we got you, though I never heard of you before. Thank you. You can go now."

The stranger looked around the room, at the shelves of books and scrolls, the platform with its inset silver circle, the table strewn with mirrors, notes, candles, and bells, and asked, "How?"

Alir blinked at him; she had never before encountered a supernatural being that didn't know how to leave. She turned to her apprentice.

"Darrend, you summoned him; I suppose you need to dismiss him."

Darrend cast her a worried look, then nodded. He gestured, and recited, "*Dagyu forrek woprei shenyu mei ganau! Empro em!*"

Nothing happened. The red-clad spirit watched the theurgists expectantly.

Alir frowned. "*Tur menadem i di ali*!" she called.

Santa Claus still stood there.

With growing urgency, the two theurgists ran through every dismissal spell they knew; then Alir started on exorcisms and wardings, which Darrend hadn't yet studied. None of them worked.

Finally, practically weeping with frustration, Alir asked, "How do you *usually* leave a place?"

"Well, usually, I've arrived by sleigh," Santa explained. "I just get back in the sleigh and give the reindeer their head."

Darrend wondered what reindeer were—apparently the word existed in Ethsharitic, since the red-clad spirit had known it immediately, and it *sounded* like an Etharitic word, but he had never heard it before.

Alir didn't worry about that. "Do you think this sleigh of yours might be nearby? Maybe we summoned that, too."

"We could look."

They did. There was no sign of a sleigh in Priest Street, or in the courtyard behind the shop—hardly surprising, since there was no snow.

"I'll check the roof," their guest suggested, stepping back inside.

"The roof? I don't…"

Alir didn't finish the sentence; instead she stared in silent amazement at the fireplace in her parlor.

The strange spirit had put a finger alongside his nose, and somehow slipped up the chimney.

Alir had never really given that chimney a close inspection, but she was quite sure the flue was far too small for so fat a man to have fit through it. Nonetheless, he had zipped up it quickly and easily.

Obviously, he did have some magic, even if he wasn't a god or a demon.

And then suddenly he came back *down* the chimney, somehow miraculously unstained by the soot in the flue, and stepped out of the fireplace. "No," he said, with a shake of his head. "They aren't up there."

"I guess we didn't get them," Darrend said.

"And you don't know any other way to get back where you belong?"

Santa Claus shook his head. "No. And…excuse me if this sounds strange, but while I was up there I looked at the sky, and the horizon—this isn't Earth, is it?"

"I'm sorry?"

"I think this is an entirely different world from the one I live on. You have a pink moon."

"Yes," Alir said.

"And an orange one," Darrend added.

"*My* world just has a big white one."

Alir and Darrend exchanged glances again. "Other worlds?" Alir sighed. "Theurgists don't *do* other worlds. For other worlds you need wizards."

"And you two aren't wizards?"

Alir drew herself up to her full height. "Certainly *not!*" she said. "We are theurgists, and proud of it!"

"Theurgists aren't wizards?" The fat man looked so puzzled that his usual smile vanished. "You're all magicians, aren't you?"

"Yes, but there are many kinds of magicians." She shrank back down a little. "And if you're really from another world, you need a wizard to get you home."

"Ah. Well, I think we'd best find a wizard, then, because millions of children are counting on me. And it's only a few…."

He paused, looking baffled again. "Sixnights? A few sixnights until *Christmas*." He shook his head. "Where I come from, we use *seven* nights, not six."

"But that's silly," Darrend said. "Seven doesn't divide evenly."

Santa laughed. "No, it doesn't, does it? Well, well."

"We need to find you a wizard," Alir said. "And if you're really in a hurry, the sooner the better." She frowned. "I just hope this isn't going to be too expensive; professional courtesy only goes so far."

"Oh, dear," Santa said. "I don't want to be a bother."

"No, it's not your fault; *my* apprentice scrambled the summoning. It's just one of the costs of doing business." She sighed. "Come on, then."

A few minutes later they were two blocks away, at a run-down shop on Wizard Street, explaining the situation to Alir's old friend Tazar the Magnificent.

"He's a spirit?" Tazar said, looking at Santa. "He looks solid enough."

"Perhaps a better word would be avatar, or incarnation," Alir said. "That's not the point. The point is that we inadvertently hauled him from his own realm to Ethshar, and now we want to send him back, and theurgy isn't suitable to the job."

Tazar nodded. He turned to the fat man. "Where are you from, then?" he asked.

"I live in a magical workshop at the North Pole," Santa replied. "On a world called Earth."

"Oh, an earth elemental? Fertility-related, perhaps?" Tazar gestured at the visitor's generous belly.

"No," Santa said. "The *world* is called Earth; *I'm* not, and I'm not the spirit of Earth. I'm a jolly old elf who brings presents to all good little boys and girls on *Christmas* morning."

Tazar frowned. "Elves are extinct in our World, and a good thing, too."

Santa looked hurt.

"Can you get him home?" Alir demanded.

Tazar sighed. "Other worlds—I hate other worlds. No, *I* can't, but I know how it can be done, if I can find someone who knows the spell." He turned. "Can you draw?" he asked the red-clad stranger. "Or even better, paint?"

Santa's usual smile returned. "Oh, certainly! I like to think I'm quite an artist, really, though I do my best work carving, rather than painting."

"Then I'll need you to paint me a picture of your home, as detailed and accurate as possible, just as it was at the instant you left. If we get it right you'll be able to step right back to it, and it will be as if you'd never been gone—well, except that you'll be a year older."

"Oh, age isn't a problem for me," Santa assured him. "But why a year older? Is that a part of the spell?"

"No," Tazar said. "But the spell takes a year to prepare."

At that, Santa, Alir, and Darrend all looked shocked and dismayed.

"And it's *very* expensive," Tazar said to Alir.

"Oh," Alir said unhappily.

When a *wizard* said something was very expensive, that implied a level of cost beyond the imagination of most people. Alir didn't have that sort of money, but she would need to find it somehow.

"It would seem you'll be my houseguest for a year," the theurgist told the red-clad spirit.

"Well, that's very kind of you," Santa said.

Alir waited for a second, hoping he would say something about payment—after all, he was supposed to be a spirit of generosity, and he had that bag, which might have valuables in it.

He didn't.

She sighed again. It looked as if she might be paying this off for the rest of her life—or at least, until Darrend completed his apprenticeship and started repaying *her* for his error.

"How are you going to send him home?" Darrend asked.

"A Transporting Tapestry," Tazar said.

That explained to Alir why it would take a year, and why they needed a picture of the destination—a wizard would have to weave a perfect life-sized image of the fat man's home, and that took time.

And that was also why it was so expensive; paying for a *full year* of a wizard's time could hardly be anything else.

"If I'm going to find someone who can do this, I had better get started," Tazar said. "And *you* should start on preparing a picture, while *you* should start raising the down-payment."

"Of course," Alir said.

"And the picture must be as exact, detailed, and accurate as you can make it," Tazar warned the fat man. "Don't let your imagination contribute anything!"

"I think I can manage," Santa said.

With that, Alir, Darrend, and Santa took their leave, and returned to Alir's shop to settle the sleeping arrangements.

Alir really, really hoped that some sort of payment would be forthcoming, and hinted broadly, but the old man paid no heed. He inspected the spare bed in the attic, and pronounced it good; he ate his share of the ham at supper with relish, and drank two pints of Alir's best beer. He accompanied Darrend down to the shops in Southgate and helped the apprentice pick out a good large board and half a dozen paints, but made no offer to pay for these materials. Throughout, he laughed and smiled; in the street he stopped several times to talk with children and ask them whether they had been behaving themselves. In general, he seemed to be having the time of his life, completely untroubled by his enforced exile.

Alir's mood, on the other hand, sank steadily as she realized just how little cash she had on hand, how few favors she could call in, and how expensive her houseguest appeared likely to be.

Over the next few days Santa spent some of his time familiarizing himself with Ethshar of the Spices and the rest working on his painting, while Alir sent Darrend out to solicit whatever business he could. Tazar searched for a weaver-wizard capable of creating the tapestry, and willing to tackle the job.

When she had a free moment, Alir watched the other-worldly spirit industriously painting a strange scene of a quaint, toy-cluttered wood-shop decorated with holly and bright red ribbons. It was still sketchy, of course, but looked quite bizarre.

One night, as Alir was once again going over her accounts and seeing no way to avoid financial ruin, the otherworldly spirit said, "You know, even if you don't have an actual *Christmas* in Ethshar, today is the fourth day of Midwinter, isn't it? Four days past the solstice? I think you might want to hang a stocking by the chimney tonight."

"I might…what?" Alir stared at him.

"Hang a stocking over the hearth."

"What are you talking…?" She stopped without completing the sentence.

He was a spirit. She was a theurgist. She was used to gods making bizarre, seemingly random demands. He claimed not to be a god, but he had appeared when summoned, like a god.

"A stocking?" she asked. "Any particular *kind* of stocking?"

"One of your own. The largest you have."

She nodded. "Hung by the hearth?"

"Above the fireplace, if possible." He blinked, as if suddenly thinking of something startling. "Open end up, toe down."

"All right," she said.

"Well, good night, then." He waved a hand, then turned and headed for the attic.

Feeling foolish, Alir found a pair of stockings that had started to lose their shape, and took one of them down to the shop, where she turned down the ankle half an inch, then hung the sock from a pothook on the chimneypiece.

It looked strange and foolish, dangling there. She stared at it, then turned up an empty palm. "The gods are mysterious," she said, as she turned and headed for her own bed.

She was awakened by Darrend gently shaking her. "Mistress?" he whispered.

She blinked sleepily.

"Mistress, I think you need to see this."

She sat up, suddenly alert and dreading whatever had driven Darrend to rouse her. "See what?"

"There's a sock…" the apprentice said.

She sagged. "Oh, is that all? I know there's a sock. I hung it there myself."

"But it's full of gold!"

Alir was not entirely sure just how she got from her bed to the hearth, still barefoot and in her nightgown, but an instant later she was staring at the stocking.

It was indeed full of gold—so full that it was gradually tearing loose from the pothook. She reached out and touched it, and the fabric tore further; she caught it with one hand as it fell, and spilled gold coins out into her other hand.

She stared at them, then smiled at Darrend.

"It would appear that our guest will be covering some of his expenses," she said.

"But why put it in a *sock?*"

"Who knows?" Alir said. "He's a god, or something like one; who knows why they do *anything* they do?"

Darrend looked at the gold, then at the stairs that led up to where their guest was sleeping. "Should we thank him?"

Alir, too, looked at the stairs. "I'm not sure," she said. "I think…well, let's just see how it goes, shall we?"

Darrend nodded.

Santa did not appear until the morning was half-over. Alir had wearied of waiting for her guest to arise, and had gone to Tazar's shop to make a long-delayed down-payment on the tapestry, so when Santa did finally descend from the attic he found Darrend sitting alone at the kitchen table.

"Ho!" he called. "How is everything this fine morning?"

The apprentice smiled at him. "Good," he said.

"Did Alir find her gift, then?"

"Yes, she did."

Santa winked at him. "You know, my lad," he said, "*Christmas* properly lasts for twelve days. Particularly when it's never been celebrated here before."

"It does?"

Santa laughed. "It really does," he said.

Darrend absorbed this, then hesitantly asked, "So should I put up a stocking, too?"

"You, and every other good boy or girl in this city!"

That didn't sound right to Darrend; what did anyone else in Ethshar have to do with this red-clad spirit? But he certainly thought *he* should put one up.

"Thank you," he said.

"Now, I believe I should finish up that painting of my workshop, don't you?"

"Yes, sir."

The fat man laughed so hard at that that his belly shook like a bowlful of...well, actually, like a bowlful of one of those nasty seafood puddings Darrend couldn't stand. Then he turned, gathered up his board and paints, and settled in a sunlit corner to finish his illustration.

When Alir returned Darrend pulled her aside, out of earshot of the fat man—or at least, he assumed it was. "Mistress," he said, "he says there are twelve days of this *Christmas* thing, and we should put up stockings again."

"Stockings? Plural?"

"One for me, and one for you." Darrend frowned. "And he said, 'and every other good boy or girl in this city.' But I don't know how he means that."

"He's a god," Alir said. "He probably means it literally." She stared thoughtfully across the room at the red-clad spirit. "That much gold could unbalance the economy, though. And why 'boy or girl,' rather than man or woman? And we don't know how he defines 'good.'" She shook her head. "I don't think we want to worry too much about that part, but perhaps we could speak to a few people. Tazar, for example."

Santa looked up from his work. "And tell them to leave the dampers open on their flues," he called. "It makes it much easier for me."

Alir and Darrend stared at him, then looked at each other, remembering how the god in red had vanished up the chimney, then come back down. "What is this thing about him and chimneys?" Darrend asked. "What does that have to do with being a spirit of giving?"

Alir turned up an empty palm. "Who knows?"

On the far side of the room Santa Claus laughed. Darrend tried not to think about that shaking belly.

The next morning Darrend hurried to the hearth to see whether the two stockings were really filled with gold. He knew that as an apprentice he would need to turn his over to his mistress, but still, the prospect of holding all that money was exciting.

And there the stockings were, bulging very promisingly—but they looked different. He frowned, and took his down. He turned it over.

No gold spilled out, but there was definitely *something* in there, something that was snagged in the fabric. Carefully, he reached in and worked it free.

It wasn't gold. It was a book, a very old, very worn little book in a soft leather binding. Darrend stared at it, and read the title inked on the cover: *How to Win Friends and Influence People*, by Deyl Karneggi, translated into Ethsharitic by Lieutenant Kelder Radler's son. Darrend opened it carefully, and read a few lines here and there; it seemed to be a collection of advice.

Very interesting advice. Darrend began reading in earnest, forgetting about the other stocking.

He was roused from his reverie by Alir's arrival. "What's that you have there?" she said.

He showed her the book. "It was in my stocking," he said.

She stared at it for a moment, then hurried to her own stocking.

"No gold," she said. "But..." She looked at the objects she had shaken out of her sock.

"What are they?" Darrend asked.

Alir shook her head. "I'm not sure," she said. "But there's a pamphlet..." She opened the little booklet. "It's instructions." She glanced at Darrend.

"Instructions for *what?*"

Alir was staring at the mysterious little cylinders and boxes. "They're cosmetics," she said. "But they aren't like any I ever saw before." She looked back at the booklet. "Hmmm."

Darrend was not very clear on the concept of cosmetics, beyond the fact that they were things rich women used to improve their appearance. He supposed it was a minor sort of magic—a branch of sorcery, perhaps, or wizardry, or maybe just herbalism. It wasn't anything that concerned him. He turned back to his book.

Later that day Alir called on Tazar, and virtually the first words the wizard said were, "How did you do that?"

"Do what?"

"This," he said, pointing at a small table by the door of his workshop.

An empty sock lay at one side of the table; beside it were several cones of bluish incense, two cut roses, a small bunch of pine needles neatly bound up in a black ribbon, and an assortment of other junk. Alir stared at this uncomprehendingly.

"It's the ingredients for the Transporting Tapestry!" Tazar said. "Some of them, anyway—we'll also need all the yarn, of course, and threads of gold and silver, and a loom. But the rest of it is right there! How did you know what was needed? How did you get it into the sock? And where did you get that incense? It's the right kind, and I didn't know there was any of it in the city! I thought we'd need to make it ourselves!"

"I didn't do anything," Alir said. "Santa did."

"Well, he's pretty amazing," Tazar said, staring at the table.

"Ten more days," Alir said, staring at the sock.

By the sixth day of *Christmas* Alir had told virtually everyone she knew about the stocking trick, and various people had received gifts of sorcerous talismans, rare and precious ingredients for spells, books on a dozen subjects, candy, coins, toys, jewelry, clothing accessories, and various other small treasures. Tazar had all the materials for the tapestry spell, and Alir, after collecting her fee for telling everyone how to obtain mysterious gifts with nothing but a sock, had paid half of the total cost.

Santa had finished his painting, and Alir stared at it in fascination. The workshop in the picture was amazingly cluttered, but still very clean. Toys and tools and devices were everywhere, most of them very alien.

The painting was delivered to Tazar, who assured Alir, Darrend, and Santa that a tapestry-capable wizard had at last been found, and that she would be starting work on the spell immediately. Tazar was as fascinated by the picture as Alir had been, and Santa began identifying and explaining the various details to the wizard. After a few moments Alir decided the conversation was going to continue all day; she made her excuses and slipped away.

Santa had not come back by the time she went to bed, but she didn't worry; after all, he could always come down the chimney. She had hung her stocking once again.

By the eleventh day of *Christmas* virtually the entire city of Ethshar of the Spices had heard about stocking magic, and the overlord had sent a magistrate to question Alir and Santa about it.

At first, neither of them understood just why the overlord was concerned; the magistrate wearily explained, "These gifts are putting a large amount of new coinage into circulation. That can affect prices. Meanwhile, certain merchants have complained that their business has suffered, because their customers have received goods from this godling without making any payment. As for all these sorcerous talismans, and potent herbs, and other magic, well, you *know* that magic is tricky stuff, no matter what form it takes. Having more of it in circulation is not helping the overlord sleep more easily."

"Oh."

"And there's the matter of fairness—one person gets a stockingful of gold, another a stockingful of candy. The obvious injustice is troubling."

"Everyone gets what they want and deserve," Santa said.

"And how is that determined, sir?" the magistrate asked.

"I have a list," Santa explained. "I know who's been naughty and who's been nice. I know when anyone writes to tell me what they want; I know what they tell family or friends."

"Naughty or nice?" The magistrate glanced at Alir, who turned up an empty palm.

"He's not from the World," she said. "I know nothing about his standards or abilities."

The magistrate frowned. "Is this stocking phenomenon going to continue indefinitely, then?"

"Oh, no!" Santa exclaimed, with a laugh. "No, no. Just one more day, and *Christmas* will be over for another year."

"And a year from now, we hope to send him back where he came from," Alir said.

"A year?"

"We're having a Transporting Tapestry made."

"I'll ask the Wizards' Guild to make that a priority."

"Thank you."

"But, sir…" Darrend began.

The magistrate turned to glare at him. "Yes, apprentice?"

"Is it really so terrible, that people are being given these little gifts? I've mostly seen happy children playing with the toys they found in their stockings, not the problems you describe. Do we really need to send him away?"

The magistrate considered for a moment, then said, "Yes."

Santa laughed. "After Twelfth Night I'll be going, then. I'll come back when the tapestry is ready."

"Wait, going?" Alir asked. "Going where?"

"North," he said. "Where I *always* go after *Christmas*."

"But…but…" Alir looked at Darrend and the magistrate.

"That will be satisfactory," the magistrate said. "I will inform the overlord."

The following morning Alir found a bottle of fine Dwomoritic wine in her stocking, and a note reading, "Thank you for your hospitality!—Santa Claus."

Santa Claus himself was gone, though; his attic bed was empty, and there was no evidence he had ever been there.

At first, Alir kept expecting the fat man in the red coat to turn up again, or at least send word, but there was no sign of him. As the months passed, she gradually turned her attention to other concerns.

It was on the first day of Midwinter that Tazar came around to Alir's shop and said, "The tapestry is almost ready; where's your spirit?"

"I don't know where he is," she admitted. "I haven't heard from him since last year."

"Well, we've put a great deal of time and effort and magic into that tapestry, so I hope it hasn't all gone to waste!"

"I'm sure it hasn't."

"If he turns up, tell him it'll be ready in a sixnight."

"Thank you, I will."

That started her thinking—where *had* Santa gone? She had heard no reports of sightings anywhere in the World. Over the next day or two she asked a few gods, but none of them admitted knowing anything about any red-garbed spirit from another world. She considered using the spell that had brought him in the first place, but summoning him when he was already somewhere in the World did not seem like a good idea.

At last, though, when she realized that it was the fourth of Midwinter, she had an inspiration. She hung a stocking on the chimneypiece, and stuffed a note in it.

She did not go to bed that night; instead she fell asleep in a chair near the hearth.

She was awakened by the sound of laughter. "Santa!" she exclaimed, sitting up.

"It's traditional to leave a glass of milk and a plate of cookies, and slip the note under the plate," he said gently. He leaned over to kiss her on the forehead. "I'll come around on the seventh, shall I?" Then he stepped quickly to the fireplace, and vanished up the chimney.

She stared at the spot where he had stood, and wondered, in her half-asleep state, how he *did* that. Then she stood up and took down her stocking.

Candy, a few unfamiliar coins, an orange—nothing of any real value, but still, she found herself smiling. She thought about eleven more days of little treasures—but then she decided not to be greedy.

Besides, in three days Santa Claus would be going home to his own world.

She wondered whether anyone else had thought to put up a stocking.

On the afternoon of the seventh of Midwinter it was snowing, and Alir was wondering whether that would keep Santa away, when there was a knock at the shop door, and Darrend opened it to let Santa in. He had his bag slung over his shoulder, and was laughing heartily. "Merry *Christmas!*" he called.

"Merry *Christmas*, Santa!" Alir replied.

They chatted for a few minutes; Santa wanted to know how business had been, how her three brothers were, and so on, and she wanted to know where he had *been* all year.

"Srigmor," he said. "And Kerroa, and Aala, and both Sardirons." Before she could ask for more details, though, he said, "Isn't there somewhere we should be going?"

"Yes, of course!"

Twenty minutes later they were in Tazar's shop, where he cautiously unveiled the tapestry.

"My goodness!" Santa exclaimed at the sight of it. "That's very realistic, isn't it?" He reached out.

"Don't touch…!" Alir began, but it was too late; the fat man in red had vanished.

For a moment the three magicians stared silently at the tapestry and the empty patch of floor where Santa had stood.

"Well, it apparently works," Tazar said at last. "You understand, we couldn't *test* it—there's no way *back*."

"Then how do you know he wound up in the right place?" Darrend demanded.

Tazar turned up an empty palm. "We don't," he said. "But if that picture was accurate, that's where he is."

"I hope it is," Alir said, staring at the image of that weird workshop.

"Well, now that he's gone, what do you want to do with the tapestry?" Tazar asked.

Alir started. "What?"

"You paid for it," Tazar explained. "It's yours. What do you want to do with it?"

"Put it away somewhere safe," she said.

"You said there's no way back?" Darrend asked.

"Somewhere *very* safe," Alir said.

Tazar nodded. "We can do that," he said.

Alir stared at the tapestry a moment longer.

She was almost tempted to reach out and touch it herself, to fling herself into that alien world that had produced Santa Claus, the world where there was an annual holiday dedicated to peace, generosity, and good will.

But it was a world without theurgists; she would be out of a job there. She turned away.

"Somewhere *very* safe," she repeated. She hesitated, glanced at the tapestry once more, then asked, "But could I have the original painting?"

ABOUT "THE UNWANTED WARDROBE"

This is the only story in the book that is not *an official Ethshar story. It is, instead, an April Fool's joke. I had written a novel called* The Unwilling Warlord, *and after a long delay I had serialized a sequel to it (and to others) that wound up with the similar title* The Unwelcome Warlock, *so for April 1, 2011, I claimed I intended to follow it up with* The Unwanted Wardrobe. *I posted alleged details describing outrageous payment terms, saying I intended to write over a hundred chapters, etc., and provided the following as the supposed first chapter. It came out well enough that I decided to include it here.*

The magic described here is all acceptable by Ethsharitic rules, as is much of the background, but some of the names aren't, and if I were to ever seriously write a story with this premise (which I might, someday) I would not jam in the Oz and Narnia references, and I'm not sure about the "Project Runway" allusion.

I'm appending some notes at the end, for those who miss the in-jokes.

THE UNWANTED WARDROBE

Chapter One

The tunic was bright purple, with red bands at the oversized cuffs and midnight-blue embroidery around the ruffled green collar. Lady Shanelle stared at it in dismay. "That totally won't work," she said. "I mean, ick. I don't want Lord Wulran to think I have *no taste at all.*"

Her friend Deyor grimaced. "Maybe you should have been more specific in what you told the wizard," she said.

"He needed to be *told* that the clothes shouldn't be hideous?" Shanelle replied. "I mean, look at that thing! No one would wear that in public."

"Maybe one of those clowns performing in the Arena would," Deyor suggested.

Shanelle glared at her. "You aren't helping."

Deyor turned up a palm. "All right, what *did* you tell the wizard? Maybe we can figure out what went wrong and find a way to fix it."

"I told him that I wanted an endless supply of beautiful clothes!"

"In exactly those words?"

Shanelle hesitated. "Well, no," she said. "Let me think." She ran her fingers through her hair. "I said…I said I wanted something that would provide me with new clothes every day, and that they should all be flawlessly made, and should all fit me perfectly, and should be designs that no one in Ethshar had ever seen before, so that I would stand out."

Deyor looked at the tunic. “Well, I think it’s safe to say no one ever saw *that* design before!”

Shanelle shuddered. “I should *hope* not.” She snatched up the tunic, wadded it into a large silken ball, and flung it into the open wardrobe. “I hope I never see it *again*!” She slammed the wardrobe door.

“You still need something to wear to the Fortress,” Deyor said.

“I know. I’ll try again.” Shanelle took a deep breath, then spoke the words that would trigger the spell anew. “*Timsez mekkitwerk*!”

A sound came from somewhere inside the wardrobe. Hesitantly, Shanelle opened the door and reached in to pull out a gown.

It was a vivid chartreuse, an ankle-length sleeveless gown with a swooping low neckline and a single shoulder strap. The skirt was slit to mid-thigh on one side, and the slit was edged with silvery lace.

“I can’t wear *that*!” Shanelle said, aghast.

“It’s not your best color,” Deyor said.

Shanelle threw her friend a dirty look, flung the dress aside, and shrieked, “*Timsez mekkitwerk*!”

This time she drew forth a pair of blue cotton breeches with heavily-stitched seams.

“All right, that’s it,” she said, glaring. “These aren’t even…I mean, they’re *breeches*! I’m a woman! And they have writing on them, on this little leather patch here—who ever heard of such a thing?”

“They’re ugly, but they look well-made,” Deyor said, looking at the garment critically. “Perhaps your brother could wear them.”

“My brother can get his own clothes! I paid fifteen rounds of gold for *my* wardrobe, not his.” She slammed the wardrobe door, and snatched the chartreuse gown off the floor. “I’m going to go show that wizard what he sold me, and give him a piece of my mind," she said. "This is *not* what I ordered." She stamped away.

Deyor paused, watching Shanelle go; then she turned thoughtfully back to the wardrobe. She looked down at the dark blue breeches that Shanelle had left lying on the bed, then said quietly, "*Timsez mekkitwerk.*" Then she cautiously opened the cabinet door.

Another tunic hung on one of the hooks. This one was shiny black, and actually looked quite presentable. Deyor carefully pulled it out and laid it on the bed. She did not recognize the fabric, and the cut was not quite like anything she had seen before, but it was quite striking. She left it on the bed while she closed the wardrobe again and whispered, "*Timsez mekkit-werk.*"

Something rustled, and she pulled forth a fringed leather skirt that had been dyed a hideous shade of red. She set it on the bed beside the black tunic and blue breeches.

Shanelle, Deyor told herself, had not thought this through. There was no reason to keep throwing rejected garments back into the wardrobe, where they would vanish; the wizard had provided her with an endless supply of new clothes, and it seemed dreadfully wasteful to keep discarding them. True, most of them had been ghastly, but every so often it produced a winner, like that black tunic, and even with the ugly ones, they were *free clothes.* They could be sold, or dyed, or taken apart for their fabric, or simply used as rags. A person could make her living off a wardrobe like this.

Of course, Shanelle was above such petty concerns as earning a living; she had her father's money to play with. Guchi the Merchant owned almost half the ships sailing out of Ethshar of the Rocks. Deyor's family, though, was not so fortunate—their pedigree went back to the Great War, when her seven-times-great grandfather had served as General Gor's quartermaster, but their wealth had dwindled over the centuries.

This piece of magical furniture might change all that, though.

"*Timsez mekkitwerk,*" Deyor murmured. "*Timsez mekkitwerk, Timsez mekkitwerk, Timsez mekkitwerk.*"

She had built a fair-sized pile on the bed when she was startled by Shanelle's voice calling, "Deyor! Aren't you coming?"

Deyor started. "Just a moment!" she answered. She looked around, but saw no alternative; she gathered up her various acquisitions and stuffed them back into the wardrobe, then turned and hurried down the stairs.

A moment later the two young women were trotting down the hill, crossing the East Road from Highside into Center City and making their way to Manolo the Blank's shop on Wizard Street.

Shanelle babbled as they walked, waving the hideous gown around, telling Deyor again how unacceptable the spell was, and how much she wanted to impress the still-unmarried Lord Wulran, because after all, the overlord wasn't actually *required* to marry a princess or another overlord's daughter, and wasn't Shanelle's own family suitably noble? Deyor said very little; she was trying to think how she might convince her wealthy friend to let her have the defective magical wardrobe. She certainly couldn't afford to pay fifteen gold rounds, but if Shanelle could somehow be made to discard it…

Then they were at Manolo's door, and Shanelle was ringing the bell, and Deyor had not thought of any way to get her hands on the wardrobe.

Manolo's apprentice Armani opened the door. "Yes?" she asked.

"We want to see the wizard," Shanelle told her.

"The wizard? But nobody can see the wizard just now."

"I *have* to see him!" Shanelle insisted.

"My orders are, nobody can see the great Manolo, not nobody, not no how."

"Why not?"

Armani's shoulders sank. "He didn't tell me that."

"Where is he? In his workshop?"

"No, he's…I don't think I should tell you."

"He's out in the garden, isn't he?" Shanelle said. "Trying to animate that statue?"

"He…he might be," Armani admitted.

"Does he *really* think it's a woman someone petrified?"

"He says he does," Armani said, somewhat defensively.

"That statue is stark naked," Shanelle said. "Who would petrify someone when she was naked?"

Armani blinked. "I…I never thought about that. Maybe whoever petrified her did it from a distance and didn't know she was naked?"

"*I* think that statue was carved by someone from ordinary stone. Someone with a dirty mind."

"Or maybe smooth skin is easier to carve than clothing," Deyor suggested.

"Maybe," Shanelle said, clearly unconvinced. "He went into plenty of detail, though."

"My master thinks it's a real woman who got petrified," Armani said. "Turning her back would be a great kindness!"

"You think he's doing it out of kindness?" Shanelle asked.

"Yes, of course!" Armani replied.

"Does he have any clothes ready for her, if he succeeds?"

"Uh…"

"Just show us to the garden," Shanelle said. "We won't interrupt his spell."

"He told me—"

"We aren't leaving until I see him," Shanelle interrupted.

Armani gave in. "This way," she said. She swung the door wide to let the two visitors into the wizard's home, and led them through the passage from the front parlor to the back gate.

They emerged into the sunny garden behind the house, where a tall iron fence separated the property from the neighbors' courtyard, and a line of statuary stood in front of the fence. There were two life-sized marble statues of handsome young men and one of a bearded patriarch dressed in the styles of a century earlier; one of a full-grown dragon was nowhere near life-sized, or it wouldn't have fit in the rather small yard. A rather overpowering wooden carving appeared to represent the goddess Piskor somewhat larger than life—or perhaps, for all Shanelle and Deyor knew, she really was nine feet tall.

At the far end of the row, beyond these and a handful of others, the wizard Manolo knelt before the next-to-last statue, a beautiful white marble female nude posed with one hand raised to her breast, fingers spread. The statue's expression was one of mild startlement, and the figure was, excluding its granite pedestal, an inch or two shorter than Shanelle.

The very last statue was of some mythological beast Shanelle and Deyor could not identify; it was vaguely catlike, but with exaggeratedly-muscular chest and forelegs, and narrow, underdeveloped hips. It had a mane of almost human-appearing hair around its face, intricately carved.

Manolo had set up a brazier between the beast and the woman, and a small cauldron hung above it, spewing forth a thick cloud of steam. Cones of incense were burning at the nude statue's feet, and an assortment of herbs and astonishingly-large feathers were elaborately arranged there, as well. The wizard's entire attention was focused on these items as he chanted something incomprehensible and waved a silver dagger through the air in intricate patterns.

Deyor held back, knowing it could be dangerous to interrupt a wizard at his work, but Shanelle strode across the garden, greenish gown in hand. "*Hai*!" she called. "Wizard!"

Manolo paid no attention as he plunged the blade of his knife into the pot of boiling water, then brought it up and flung several drops on the statue. "*Pyrzqxgl*!" he shouted.

There was a shimmer, and the air seemed to change color for an instant; then the statue's white surface began to melt away, revealing black hair and light brown skin.

"Ha!" Manolo exclaimed. "I *told* them it was too accurate for a mere carving!"

Deyor stared in amazement as the woman who had been a statue a moment before gradually returned to life, blinking in surprise and turning to look at her surroundings.

Shanelle, however, paid no attention as she stamped up to the wizard. "*Hai*!" she said, waving the gown. "I'm talking to you! Unhappy customer here!"

"What?" Manolo turned, startled, as he finally realized he was not alone in the garden—or rather, that he and the former statue were not alone.

"That wardrobe you sold me!" Shanelle shouted. "Do you have any *idea* how hideous the stuff it's making is?"

The former statue turned to stare at the wizard and his angry customer. "Where am I?" she asked. "Who are you people?"

Manolo smiled at her, and bowed. "I am Manolo the Blank, master wizard," he said. "I have just reversed a petrifaction spell someone cast on you long ago."

"Wizard!" Shanelle demanded.

Annoyed, Manolo turned to her. "Could you wait for just a moment, please? I have just rescued this lovely woman from a fate worse than death, by means of a very dangerous eighth-order spell, and I would like to have a few words with her. I will attend to your complaint shortly."

"You'd better," Shanelle said. She glared at the naked woman. "Who are you, anyway, and who turned you to stone?"

"My name is Vweeton," she said. "I assume it was the wizard Ballensyagga who petrified me—he objected to having to compete with a witch for business."

Shanelle looked dubious. "What kind of a name is Vweeton?" she demanded. She turned to Manolo. "You know, I don't think she was petrified at all; I think your magic brought a real statue to life."

"Oh, no," Manolo said. "Javan's Restorative won't do that. Here, look." He dipped the dagger in the pot again and flung a few drops at the beast statue. "*Pyrzqxgl*," he said.

The air flickered, and the white surface began to dissolve, revealing tawny fur; Manolo's mouth fell open in astonishment. "But it can't!" he said. "That's an imaginary monster!"

"What, the lion?" Vweeton said, stepping down from her pedestal. "No, it's not imaginary; why would you think that?" She walked toward the emerging beast and reached out a calming hand. "You might want to find some way to restrain him, though. I can keep him happy with my witchcraft for awhile, but I'm eventually going to get tired, and he's going to get hungry, and yes, he'll happily eat people."

"Augh!" Manolo said, backing away.

"You might also find me some clothes," the witch said, as she petted the lion's head. "I suppose Ballensyagga caught me in my bath—at least, the last thing I remember is hearing a noise as I got out of the tub."

Manolo looked around and saw the gown draped on Shanelle's arm. "What's that?" he asked.

"*That*," Shanelle said, "is why I'm here. It's hideous! Your magic wardrobe is turning out the ugliest clothes I've ever seen!"

"It's still better than nothing," Vweeton said. "Toss it here."

Shanelle obeyed. "Go ahead and put it on, if you want," she said, "but don't blame me if you look like a clown."

Vweeton stepped away from the lion and untangled the dress, then pulled it over her head, tugged it down, and settled it on her hips. She looked down at it critically.

Shanelle, Deyor, Armani, and Manolo stared. The chartreuse that had looked so ghastly in Shanelle's bedroom went surprisingly well with the witch's brown skin, and the absurd single shoulder was oddly fetching.

"You know," Deyor said, after a long moment of silence, "on you, it looks good."

Notes:

All the characters who appear in the story are named for fashion icons:

Shanelle = Chanel
Deyor = Dior
Guchi = Gucci
Manolo the Blank = Manolo Blahnik
Armani = Armani
Vweeton = Vuitton
Ballensyagga = Balenciaga

General Gor, Lord Wulran, Javan, and Piskor the Generous are established figures in Ethshar's history, and the geography (this is set in Ethshar of the Rocks) is accurate and consistent with all other Ethshar stories.

In case you didn't pick up on it, the "blue breeches" are a pair of jeans.

"*Timsez mekkitwerk*" = "Tim says, make it work," a reference to Tim Gunn's signature line on TV's "Project Runway."

"*Pyrzqxgl*" is the magic word used by Kiki Aru to transform himself and others in L. Frank Baum's *The Magic of Oz.*

Armani's initial refusal to admit the visitors to see the wizard is modeled on a scene in MGM's 1939 film of "The Wizard of Oz."

And I trust the presence of a lion, a witch, and a wardrobe requires no explanation.

About "The Warlock's Refuge"

Back in the 1990s I wrote Night of Madness, *describing how warlockry first arrived in the World, and how an accommodation was reached between these new magicians and the existing society. That story introduced Lord (later Chairman) Hanner, and established how the Calling worked. It also showed how there might be an obvious way to* avoid *the Calling. Clearly, I needed to explain why warlocks never exploited this, so I plotted "The Warlock's Refuge." I didn't actually get around to writing it for a decade or so, though. I only finally did so because I needed readers to be familiar with it before tackling the novel that eventually became* The Unwelcome Warlock. *I had been planning that story (then called* The Final Calling*) since the 1980s, but kept putting it off, as there were all these other pieces that I thought should be done first, such as* The Vondish Ambassador *and "The Warlock's Refuge."*

I did get to it eventually. "The Warlock's Refuge" was published on my website in April of 2010, and then republished as Chapter One of The Unwelcome Warlock, *and here it is again.*

THE WARLOCK'S REFUGE

Hanner the Warlock looked at the tapestry without really seeing it; that constant nagging whisper was distracting him. He closed his eyes for a moment to clear his thoughts, but that seemed to make it worse. He clenched his jaw, shook his head, and balled his hands into fists.

"Is this not what you had in mind, Chairman?"

The wizard's voice brought Hanner back to reality for a moment. He opened his eyes and forced himself to focus on the tapestry.

The silky fabric hardly seemed to be there at all; the image woven into the cloth was so detailed, so perfect, that he seemed to be looking through the tapestry into a world beyond, rather than at the material itself.

In that world gentle golden sunlight washed across a green hillside strewn with wild flowers beneath a clear blue sky above. In the distance he could make out a cluster of handsome golden-tan buildings, though details were vague.

"Does it work?" he asked.

The wizard beside him glanced at the tapestry. "It does," Arvagan said. "My apprentice tested it before I sent for you. The tapestry that can return you to Ethshar is hanging in that house there, on the right." He pointed, but was careful to keep his finger well back from the cloth—the slightest contact would trigger the tapestry's magic and pull him into that other world.

"The tapestry that comes out in the attic of Warlock House?"

"Precisely."

"And these tapestries will work for warlocks?"

The wizard hesitated. "I *think* so," he said at last. "You understand, without a warlock's cooperation we have no way of testing it. Divinations are unreliable where warlocks are concerned. We know *some* tapestries work for warlocks, and I don't see any reason these wouldn't, but magic is tricky."

That brief hesitation had been enough for the Calling to once again start to work on Hanner; he had turned his head away from the tapestry as if to listen to the wizard's reply, but then the motion had continued, and now he was staring over the wizard's left shoulder, to the north, toward Aldagmor.

He needed to go there, and soon. He needed to forget about all this Council business, forget about the wizards and their tapestries, forget about schemes to avoid the Calling. He needed to forget about Mavi and their children, and about his sisters and his friends, and about the other members of the Council of Warlocks, and just *go.* Whatever was up there in Aldagmor, it needed him, and he needed to go to it…

"Chairman?"

Hanner bit his lip. What he *needed*, he told himself as he forced himself back to reality, was a refuge where he couldn't hear the Calling, couldn't feel its constant pull.

And that was what these tapestries were supposed to provide. That was what he had paid the Wizards' Guild eight thousand rounds of gold to obtain, a fortune that had completely wiped out his own assets, and half the Council's money as well.

"I'm sorry," he said. "What were you saying?"

"I was saying that we do not actually know whether this tapestry will do what you wanted. We don't understand your magic, any more than you understand ours, and we have no way of testing how those two magics will interact, other than sending a warlock through the tapestry. We know that warlocks have used *other* tapestries safely, but wizardry can be…erratic. We can't promise what *this* tapestry will do until a warlock tries it."

"You haven't tested that?"

"Chairman Hanner, you specifically forbade us from telling any other warlock anything about this project. That was part of our contract, and we have abided by it."

"Of course," Hanner said. "I didn't want to get anyone's hopes up. So you don't know whether I will be able to hear the Calling from that other world?"

"Chairman, we have no idea what the Calling is. No, we don't know how it works, or whether it extends into the new universe we created for you. We know that you can breathe the air there, and drink the water, and that my apprentice suffered no ill effects from doing so. We know he chewed on a blade of grass and wasn't poisoned. We know that the village in the tapestry was uninhabited when he got there, though we can't say with any certainty whether its builders, if it *was* built, might still be around somewhere. We know he says that he walked three or four miles around the area without finding any people, or any animals larger than a rabbit, or any edge to the world he was in. But that's about it as far as our knowledge goes. We don't know whether warlockry will operate there. We don't know whether there are natives dwelling somewhere in that world. We don't even know how long the day is there—he didn't stay long enough to determine that. Creating worlds is an unpredictable business, Chairman; we told you that when we first agreed to this."

"You did," Hanner admitted.

This had been a tremendous gamble, paying the wizards to create a world, and there was only one way to find out whether it had worked, or whether he had thrown away an immense fortune for nothing. All he had to do was reach out and touch the tapestry, step into it, and he would be in that other world, that beautiful refuge.

He started to raise his hand, then stopped.

"Not here," he said. "I might not..."

He didn't finish the sentence; when he realized what he had been going to say, he forced himself to stop.

He had been about to say he couldn't use the tapestry because it might cut him off from the Calling, but that was what he had wanted; that was the whole *point*. This tapestry was intended to let warlocks escape from the doom that eventually befell them all.

Every warlock knew that the farther he was from Aldagmor, the weaker the Calling was—and the weaker his magic was, as well, but that was only a secondary consideration. That weakening had given Hanner the idea to find, or make, a place so distant from Aldagmor than the Call couldn't reach it at all.

The Calling reached to every corner of the World; warlocks had established that. From sun-baked Semma in the southeast to frozen Kerroa in the northwest, there was no place in the World where a warlock was safe.

So obviously, the warlocks needed a refuge that wasn't in the World at all, and that meant they needed wizardry. The only three kinds of magic that could reach out of the World into other places were demonology, theurgy, and wizardry—herbalism, witchcraft, ritual dance, and the rest were limited to everyday reality.

The gods didn't recognize warlocks as human beings, and had trouble even acknowledging their existence, so theurgy wasn't going to help. The Nethervoid, where demons originated, wasn't anywhere anyone would ever want to go, and trusting demons was usually a stupid thing to do, so demonology was out, too. That left wizardry. Wizards had various spells that could reach other planes of existence. It wasn't clear whether these spells opened a path to places that had existed all along, or created new places out of nothing, but they could definitely provide access to other worlds. Hanner had even visited one, long ago, and found that warlockry did not work there, and that presumably the Calling did not reach it.

And here it was, the wizardry he had asked for—a Transporting Tapestry to another world that just might be the refuge the warlocks needed.

It looked lovely, but that didn't mean much. Arvagan's apprentice had survived a visit there, so it couldn't be *too* hostile, but would it really be a decent place to live? Would it be a safe home for his wife and children?

He grimaced at that. He was assuming that Mavi would want to accompany him, but he had not actually asked her yet. He knew she was worried about the Call, but worried enough to give up her life in Ethshar of the Spices, the city that had always been her home? It wasn't as if *she* was in any danger; he had invited her to become a warlock, to have that little adjustment made that would let her draw magical power from the Source, but she had never done it. She was content to leave the magic to him and the other warlocks while she attended to more mundane matters.

But she loved him, and wanted to be with him, so of course she would want to come with him. She wouldn't need to stay; she could go back and forth at will, while he would need to remain in that other place once the Calling became too strong.

That assumed, of course, that it wasn't just as strong on the other side of the tapestry. He really would need to try it out someday, when the Call reached a dangerous level—maybe after he got back from Aldagmor…

He closed his eyes and clenched his teeth and held his breath.

He was *not* going to Aldagmor. He was not going to give in. The Call was obviously already dangerous. It was always there, every second, day and night, nagging at him, working insidiously to draw him away. Every time he used even the slightest bit of warlockry, or took a single step to the north, it grew a little stronger. Simply facing south was becoming difficult; his head kept turning involuntarily, and his neck was getting sore from his struggle to resist. He was leaking magic, he knew that; small objects tended to levitate around him without any conscious effort on his part. He *needed* a refuge.

And now, just in time, he might have one. All he had to do was reach out…

But the wizards didn't know, didn't *really* know, whether it was safe, or whether it would work. He should go home and discuss it with his wife before he did anything more. He should go home, just a mile north of this secret room on Wizard Street.

A mile *north*. A mile closer to Aldagmor.

It was very bad. He wasn't going to be able to hold out much longer. He couldn't sleep anymore; when he did, he dreamed of fire and of being cast down from the heavens and buried deep in the earth of Aldagmor, he dreamed of a need to go there and help, and he always awoke to find himself moving northward. He hadn't dared to sleep at all for the last two nights, and he had made do with brief naps for a sixnight before that.

He just had to reach out and touch the tapestry, but he couldn't lift his hand. He was so tired, so weary; if he gave in he could rest. He could fly, any warlock worthy of the name could fly, he could be in Aldagmor in no more than a day or two. He had been refusing to fly for about a month, so that he would not fly off to Aldagmor, but now that just seemed foolish. Why not get it over with?

"Tell my wife I love her," he said. "Tell her to wait for me in Warlock House attic. If this works, I'll meet her there and let her know. If it doesn't, well…"

"Should we tell her any details? About the tapestries?"

Hanner shook his head. "No," he said. "I'll tell her. She knows I was planning something, and I want to be the one to tell her what it was." He paused, then added, "If it works. For all we know, the Call will be even stronger in there."

"I suppose it might be," Arvagan admitted. "Though I don't see why it would be. Wherever that place is, it's not Aldagmor."

"But it could be *near* Aldagmor, somehow."

"I suppose."

Hanner turned to Arvagan. "You'll tell her?"

"The instant I see you enter the tapestry, I'll send word for her to go to meet you."

"Good. Good." He turned back to face that shining image of green fields, and tried to step toward it, but his foot would not lift.

Inspiration struck. "Arvagan, would you do me a favor?"

"What sort of a favor?"

"Would you move the tapestry to the north wall? Or just turn it so it faces south?"

"Is it that bad, Chairman?"

"Yes, it is," Hanner said. "I didn't know…It took so long…"

"We told you when we started that it took a year or more to make a Transporting Tapestry."

"Yes, you did—but I hadn't realized how close I was to being Called. A year ago it was nothing, just a little murmur in my head; now it's…it's everything, it's constant, it's so *strong*."

Arvagan nodded. Then he reached up and pushed at the rod supporting the tapestry, being careful not to let his hand come too close to the fabric. Like the sail of a ship clearing the breakwater, the tapestry swung slowly around.

Hanner turned with it, and when it was due north, between him and Aldagmor, he found he could lift his arm and step forward, step northward. His finger touched the silky cloth.

And the secret room was gone, the wizard's house was gone, Wizard Street and the Wizards' Quarter had vanished, the entire city of Ethshar of the Spices was gone. He was standing on a gentle, grassy slope.

He didn't notice.

A sun was shining warmly on his face, a sun that wasn't quite the same color as the one he had seen every day in Ethshar, and a soft wind was blowing against his right cheek; he didn't notice that, either.

Sky and sun and wind and grass, a sound of splashing somewhere in the distance, a cluster of strange buildings—Hanner ignored them all.

He was too busy listening to the silence in his head.

The Call was *gone*. The constant nagging, the murmuring voice in his head, the wordless muttering that he had somehow been able to draw magic from, was gone. There was nothing in his head but *him*.

He hadn't experienced such total mental freedom since the Night of Madness, more than ten years before. Even before he had consciously noticed it, he had lived with the whisper of magic constantly for so long that its absence was overwhelming. Now he simply stood, listening for it, for several minutes.

At first he didn't show any reaction; the change was too sudden, too complete, to comprehend. Then the rush of relief swept over him, and his knees gave way, and he tumbled onto the grass, trembling with the impact of his release from bondage—and trembling with terror, as well. His magic was gone, and it had been central to his existence for so long that he barely knew who he was without it.

He lay on the grass for several minutes, and gradually began to notice his surroundings—the sun, the breeze, the grassy slope. He tried to stand up.

It didn't work.

He took a moment to absorb that, and to realize that he had become so accustomed to levitating any time he stood up that trying to rise using only his own muscles was difficult, surprisingly difficult. He had forgotten how to do it.

He had tried to spring directly to his feet—or really, since of late he had usually hung in the air with his feet an inch or so off the ground, "to his feet" wasn't quite right. He had tried to fling himself upright, but without magic it hadn't worked. Now he rolled onto his back and pushed himself up into a sitting position, then set his feet on the ground, one by one. Then he stood up, leaning forward and straightening his legs.

That time it worked.

He stood for a moment, taking in his surroundings and his situation.

He had no magic. Wherever he was, he wasn't a warlock here; probably nobody would be. All the little things he had done magically he either had to do with his own muscles, or not at all.

He was dismayed to realize how many of them there were. He had been using warlockry to stand up, to walk—or rather, to fly; he realized now he hadn't actually *walked* in months. He had been summoning things to his hand, rather than reaching out to take them. Magic had infiltrated every part of his life. Now that his head was clear he could remember any number of ways he had used magic—walking, lifting, cooking, cleaning, heating, cooling, playing with his children, even making love to his wife. He had done it all without thinking. Even when he had begun to feel the Call, when his dreams had become nightmares and the whisper in his head had become a constant nagging, and he had tried to stop using warlockry because it made him more susceptible, he had unconsciously continued doing all those little, everyday magics. The power *wanted* to be used, so he had used it.

And only now that he *couldn't* use it did he realize he had been doing so. He was standing here on a grassy hillside, and his legs were supporting his entire weight, his skin was unprotected from sun and wind, and it felt *strange*.

He thought he could get used to it, though. After all, he hadn't been born a warlock; he had grown to adulthood without any magic. Most people managed just fine without warlockry.

He sniffed the air, and caught the scent of the sea, or something very like it. He walked cautiously down toward the cluster of buildings that he could not help thinking of as a village, though he had no idea whether that was really an accurate description.

As he drew near he decided that they were indeed houses, and did indeed comprise a village. They were built of some hard, golden-brown material—stone or brick or dried mud, he couldn't tell which. There were many small windows, and a few arched doorways. Arvagan had said that the builders might not be human, but the proportions looked right for humans; Hanner didn't see anything particularly odd about the houses.

Beyond the village the land continued to fall away, and he could see the ocean, or something very like it, spreading out in the distance. A tree-lined stream gurgled its way past the village, which accounted for the splashing he had heard, and the leaves rustled in the gentle breeze.

It was very pleasant, really. Arvagan had said that he couldn't guarantee anything about this place, that there might be hidden dangers, anything from insidious poisons to rampaging monsters to distorted time, but to Hanner it looked calm and inviting. The stream would presumably provide water, and the land looked fit for growing food; there might be fish in the sea, or even clams to be dug along the shore.

Or if appearances were deceiving, and that somehow proved impossible, if the tapestries continued to work as promised he could still have food and even water brought in from Ethshar.

Unless there were some nasty surprises awaiting him, he had his refuge—a place where warlocks could come to escape the Calling.

He wandered around for what felt like an hour or so, exploring the houses. They were largely unfurnished, as if their intended inhabitants had never arrived, never brought their belongings.

That was fine. That was *perfect.*

The air was sweet, the sun was warm, and there was no Call. It was everything Hanner had wanted.

And in one house, just as Arvagan had said, was the other tapestry, the one depicting the attic of Warlock House that had once belonged to Hanner's uncle, Lord Faran. That bare, dim room looked dismal compared to the bright sunlit refuge, but Hanner did not hesitate; he knew his wife was waiting for him there. Mavi and the children had been worried about him; this refuge would be a relief for them all, even if none of the others ever set foot in it. Hanner walked up to the tapestry, and put a hand and a foot out to touch it, eager to tell Mavi the good news.

He knew the Calling would return, but he assumed it would take a few seconds to reach its old force. He thought he was ready for it.

Then he was in the attic, back home in Ethshar of the Spices, and he was wrong. There was no delay at all. The Call was instantaneously a deafening, irresistible screaming in his head, and he had had no time to prepare, no chance to brace himself; after an hour of freedom his resistance was gone, and he could not restore it quickly enough. There was one final instant of clarity, one glimpse of Mavi waiting, staring at him as he appeared out of thin air, and then there was no room in his mind for any thought but the desperate need to get to Aldagmor as fast as he could, by any method he could. Nothing could be permitted to stand in his way, and with a wave of his hand he shattered the sloping ceiling, splitting the rafters and tearing wood and tile to shreds as he soared out into the sky. He could not spare so much as a second to tell his wife goodbye before flying northward.

He did not hear Mavi call his name, did not hear her burst into tears as he vanished. He did not see Arvagan's apprentice rush up the attic stairs to her side, to catch her before she collapsed.

By the time the apprentice brought Mavi to Arvagan's shop, Hanner was thirty leagues from the city. By the time word went out to the Council of Warlocks, Hanner was in Aldagmor. He could not tell them what had happened. He could not tell them that the refuge was a success, and only failed because he had been caught off-guard by the sudden instantaneous return of a Calling he had only barely been able to resist *before* he stepped through the tapestry.

All they knew was that Hanner, Chairman of the Council, had stepped through the Transporting Tapestry still able to fight the Call, and upon emerging had instantly flown off to Aldagmor.

There were some who theorized that the Call was somehow stronger on the other side of the tapestry, some who thought the magic of the tapestry itself somehow added to the Call's power, some who really didn't care about the details, but the Council as a whole agreed: The Chairman's attempt at creating a safe haven for high-level warlocks had failed. The tapestry was rolled up and stored securely away—after all, it was bought and paid for—and a new Chairman was elected.

And the Calling, that inexplicable melange of nightmares and compulsions, continued to snatch away any warlock who grew too powerful.

ABOUT "THE FROG WIZARD"

Okay, this one needs some explanation, as it's never been published in this form before.

Long ago I bought a blank book, wrote and illustrated a story in it, and gave it to my girlfriend for Valentine's Day. Then later, when she had more or less forgotten about it, I stole it back and wrote and drew another story in it, and gave it to her for Valentine's Day. I did this until the book was full—not every year, but most.

They weren't romantic stories; they were silly children's stories. One of them was called "The Frog Wizard."

Many, many years later, after the book was long since full and she and I were long since married, I read some of the stories to our kids, and it occurred to me that a couple of them might be worth reworking and selling. I proceeded to rewrite "The Frog Wizard" in several versions—six in all. One of them was an Ethshar version. I actually sold one of the other versions, though; it was published in the January 1993 issue of **Science Fiction Age**. *The Ethshar version was shelved and forgotten about—until I started assembling this book, when I realized that if I was going to be complete, it needed to be included. So here it is, a technically-never-before-published Ethshar story. And yes, it's canon; the wizard's spell is a variant form of Llarimuir's Mass Transmogrification, and Mreghon is in the northwestern Small Kingdoms.*

THE FROG WIZARD

Long ago, in the Small Kingdoms, in the most easterly corner of a land called Mreghon, there lived a wizard whose name is forgotten.

He never used it much in any case, since a wizard's true name gives power to other wizards who know it, and any name used often enough might become a true name. His neighbors were generally content to simply call him "the wizard," and he was content to be called that.

However, as it happens, he was not really very much of a wizard, despite his best efforts. No matter what he did, no matter how hard he tried, no matter how much he studied, he could work only one single piece of real, genuine magic.

His neighbors were not aware of this shortcoming, because he was very good at sleight-of-hand and at all manner of stunts that *looked* like wizardry. He could convince anyone who dropped by that he knew all manner of fine spells, could make small objects appear and disappear, could transform handkerchiefs into pigeons, and so forth.

Sleight-of-hand is all very well, of course, but it's not quite the same thing as true wizardry, and the wizard knew it. True wizardry means miracle-working, not putting a pigeon up your sleeve, and this wizard only knew one genuine wizard's spell, which he had learned as an apprentice—to the utter astonishment of his master, who had been trying to teach him an entirely different spell. The master could not manage anything of the sort himself, and did not understand how his apprentice had ever discovered it.

When spells for flying or fire-lighting failed regularly, when his love-charms just gave people belly-aches, when a simple geas made a smelly mess all over his carpet without even making the intended victim feel guilty about it, this one feat came easily to the wizard. He could do it instantly, just with a wave of his hand.

It wasn't a simple, ordinary spell, either, like fire-lighting or levitation—he couldn't light a candle by wizardry for all the gold in a dragon's hoard, but somehow he had mastered, without meaning to, a truly spectacular piece of magic. Perhaps some perverse minor deity had been having a joke with him in allowing him the easy use of this major transformation.

He could turn people into frogs.

A simple gesture, and anyone he chose would shrink down, turn green and slimy, and hop away, eager to eat bugs, as much a frog as any frog that ever grew out of a tadpole. He could transform any number of people at a time, too, for that matter—turn whole nations into frogs, if he chose to.

He didn't choose to, however, and for a very good reason indeed. Unfortunately, he couldn't turn the frogs back into people again, and after one or two unpleasant incidents that took place before he fully realized the situation, he swore never to use the spell again. He was too soft-hearted, in the ordinary course of events, to leave even his worst enemy stuck forever in the form of a frog.

He practiced the gesture in secrecy, just in case he ever needed it, but he never used it.

He still wanted everyone to know he was a wizard, though. There were a good many magicians living in Mreghon at the time, wizards and sorcerers and theurgists and a variety of others—the exact reasons for this are unclear, but indisputably, Mreghon had more than its share of practitioners of the arts arcane. These magicians were something of a privileged elite, highly respected by the rest of the population, and deferred to in several ways. A known magician could always count on a fair price at the village market, and no smith would ever miss the promised delivery date on a wizard's or sorcerer's order.

After all, angering a wizard is dangerous. He might turn you into a frog. Everyone knew that, even though in truth, most wizards didn't know that particular spell.

That this one wizard *did* know it, and had mastered it so completely without ever learning any more useful or benign magic, was a source of constant private irritation, but really, the wizard had no choice but to live with it.

And since he *had* mastered this spell, and really *could*, if he chose, turn people into frogs, he played the role of a wizard to the hilt. He wore a fancy hat and embroidered robe, with a silver dagger on his belt; he carried an ornately-carved staff with a cat's skull on top, and lived in a well-furnished cave rather than an ordinary house to add to his mystique. He collected and studied various old books—partly in hopes of learning more magic, but mostly just to keep up his image. He kept strange pets, such as lizards and giant spiders—nothing supernatural, though, since he had no way of manufacturing, summoning, or controlling such creatures. He equipped himself with a full wizard's laboratory, crammed with all the usual bizarre paraphernalia—skulls, stuffed bats, mysterious powders, all of that—even though he couldn't use a single bit of it.

In short, he did everything a powerful wizard did, except to perform any genuine wizardry.

Reasonably enough, everyone in the vicinity assumed he was a great and powerful wizard.

As a sort of private reference to his peculiar situation, he wore green robes instead of the more traditional red or blue or gold, and he had a silver frog emblazoned on his hat. Accordingly, when people needed to distinguish him from the other wizards in the area, they referred to him as "the frog wizard."

This was all very well, and in fact it was exactly what the frog wizard wanted. He led a quiet, comfortable life, and had the respect and affection of his neighbors. Really, he was quite content with the situation.

Unfortunately, it didn't last, because late one summer Mreghon was invaded.

The first the frog wizard knew of this was when a messenger knocked on the door of his cave one fine morning, carrying a royal summons from King Kelder, the monarch of Mreghon.

The wizard was sitting in the parlor with his feet up, sipping tea and reading a tome on the best substitutes for dragon's blood in assorted fire spells, when he heard a loud, impatient rapping. He sighed, put the book aside, and got to his feet.

The rapping sounded again, and he answered the door, expecting to see one of his neighbors come looking for a bit of advice, or maybe some villager asking after a philtre of some sort.

Instead he found himself face to face with a royal herald, in the full ceremonial regalia of his office.

The wizard blinked, startled, and before he had time to do any more than blink the herald had unrolled a scroll and begun reading. The wizard stood there, feeling rather foolish, and listened.

The herald proclaimed in a deep, rolling voice, "Whereas, Our Realm has been attacked, without provocation, by certain Enemies, and…"

The herald took a deep breath, and the wizard started to say something, but before he could get a single sound out the herald continued, "Whereas, Our normal methods of defense do not appear to provide a complete assurance of Victory against this foul invader, and…"

Again a deep breath, and a continuation.

"Whereas, supernatural methods needs must be employed against this Desecration of Our Borders, and…"

Another deep breath.

"Whereas, Our enlightened rule has provided all alike, commoner and noble, mortal and magician, with great benefits and fair treatment..."

The herald paused dramatically, one hand raised, and the wizard waited politely.

"*Therefore*," the herald announced, "We call upon all those with any skills in arcane practices, be they in wizardry, sorcery, theurgy, witchcraft, or other practices, to recognize their obligation to the Crown, *and...*"

The wizard really wished that the herald would forget about the dramatic pauses and get on with it.

"*Therefore*, all practitioners of Magic are hereby summoned forthwith to the Castle Royal, by Command of His Majesty Kelder, First of That Name, Heir to the Ancient Lords of the Holy Kingdom of Ethshar."

The herald nodded for emphasis, and began rolling up the scroll as he concluded, "Signed, and with Our Seal, this fourteenth day of the month of Harvest, in the Year of Human Speech Five Thousand and Sixty-Eight."

The wizard was very impressed by all this, which sounded quite majestic, and when the herald had finished reading the wizard asked him just exactly what it all meant.

"It means that you're to come with me to the castle, immediately," the herald explained.

The wizard considered that for a moment, and then asked, "Why?"

"You're a wizard, aren't you?" the herald asked.

The wizard promptly agreed that yes, he was indeed a wizard.

"Well," the herald explained, "all the magicians in Mreghon are being summoned to the castle to help fight off the invader."

The wizard was not at all sure he liked the sound of that, and he said so.

The herald insisted, and made some rather nasty threats about what the king might do to uncooperative magicians.

The wizard remarked that it was all very unfair.

The herald argued that the invasion was unfair, and it wasn't the king's fault, and it didn't really matter whose fault it was or whether it was fair or not, because it all came out the same in the end—the wizard had to come to the castle if he didn't want to be in a very great deal of trouble.

The wizard continued to argue for awhile, but the herald was relentless in his insistence.

In the end, the wizard gave in on the major points, but he did a little insisting of his own and was allowed time to pack a bag and finish his tea.

While he was packing, and on the walk to the castle, he asked the herald more questions, and got more of an explanation of just what was going on.

It seems that the exact reason for the invasion was not entirely clear to the Mreghonians, but it appeared to have something to do with an insult the Mreghonian king, Kelder the First, had unintentionally directed at the king of Lassuron, a surly fellow by the name of Bardec who had a reputation for turning every little incident into a war, and who had thus enlarged Lassuron considerably at the expense of its neighbors—such as tiny Mreghon.

Although the insult was completely inadvertent, King Bardec had chosen to take umbrage—he had probably been looking for an excuse. He had led an army of some four hundred men into Mreghon, marching them through the peaceful countryside, burning farmhouses and trampling crops and in general making life very unpleasant for the citizenry.

The year had already been a bad one for the Mreghonians, as the wizard well knew. Some quirk of the weather had cursed the kingdom with a veritable plague of gnats and mosquitoes, the crops had been poor, several wells had gone dry at midsummer, and then a few sixnights later heavy rains had caused flooding along the little river that trickled through Mreghon on its way to the Gulf of the East.

After all this, most people were not really surprised by the attack. As everyone knows, bad luck often comes in streaks. Some people had wondered if they had offended some god or other, but most just put it down to chance and accepted it as another nuisance to be tolerated.

To some, it was rather more than just a nuisance. Naturally, King Kelder was quite upset by the invasion. The kingdom had been at peace for years, and the minuscule standing army was out of shape, out of practice—and out building levees against the floods.

Even in the best of times, the Mreghonian army was probably no match for King Bardec's force, and as it stood, defeat had appeared certain. From King Kelder's point of view that was completely unacceptable; King Bardec had announced that his honor had been impugned by poor Kelder, and that only a direct personal duel to the death between the two monarchs would satisfy him. As Bardec was young, fit, and famous for his skill with a broadsword, while Kelder was aging, fat, lazy, and inept, this was the same as stating that he intended to kill the Mreghonian king.

Ordinarily, the Small Kingdoms being as small as they are, King Bardec and his army could have reached King Kelder's castle in a few hours' march, and the war would have been over within a day. In this particular case, however, Mreghon was blessed with an ally. Serem of Fileia was the father of the current queen of Mreghon, and did not care to see his daughter widowed. He had distracted King Bardec with elaborate diplomatic maneuvers that had been ultimately unfruitful, but which had gotten the Lassuronian army marched off in entirely the wrong direction for a day or two as an honor guard for the ceremonies.

King Kelder had taken this respite as an opportunity to review his situation, and to realize just how pitiful his defenses were. He saw plainly that if he wanted to survive, he had to find some way to defeat King Bardec without an army. Obviously, that would take a miracle—and that meant magic.

Accordingly, King Kelder had sent messengers out, and posted proclamations, and did everything he could to locate and gather every magician in Mreghon. When they had been located, he summoned one and all, however powerful or puny, to his castle.

And that, of course, included this frog wizard.

The wizard had been staying inside lately, because of the mosquitoes, and had missed all news of the invasion—until now.

He really did not want to be involved in a war, but he did not see any practical way to back out, so he went along with the herald without any serious argument.

It was a beautiful sunny day, and the worst of the summer's heat had passed, leaving a gentle breeze that blew the clouds about like gamboling sheep, but the frog wizard was unable to enjoy any of it while worrying about what lay ahead.

Soon enough they reached the royal castle, and hurried across the drawbridge into the great hall, where the wizard was introduced around, checked off a long list of magicians who were expected, and then generally made welcome by the castle staff.

He wanted none of this welcome. He promptly found a quiet corner and did his best to stay there, out of the way, while the messengers and heralds brought in magician after magician—witches, sorcerers, wizards, magicians of every sort.

The frog wizard recognized several of them, while others were total strangers, but he said nothing to any of them. He just sat and watched them arrive—and they kept on coming, and coming, and coming.

He was quite amazed. Really, he had had no idea that there were so *many* magicians in Mreghon! They kept on arriving, off and on, for the next two days.

Throughout that two days the frog wizard generally stayed in his corner, trying hard to be inconspicuous, and succeeding, for the most part. He slept on a mat in a magicians' barracks that had been improvised in a gallery, and he ate the bread and cheese and ale that the castle servants distributed three times a day, but other than that he simply sat quietly and watched and waited.

On the third day the magicians stopped coming. Instead, the invaders appeared and surrounded the castle.

By this time, though, the castle was full of magicians, dozens of magicians, magicians of every description, marching about and boasting of their prowess.

King Bardec's army arrived at the castle about midday and, as expected, found the drawbridge up and the battlements manned—they had no way of knowing that the defenders were the castle servants, rather than soldiers, nor that the place was crammed with magicians.

The invaders spread out and settled in for a proper siege, setting up tents and pavilions, bringing up a battering ram, and so forth.

Meanwhile, inside the castle, the magicians were milling about, unsure just what was expected of them. After the initial round of silly boasting, most of them found they had little to say to one another, and nothing at all to do.

Around sunset King Kelder finally appeared in the great hall, in his best royal robes and wearing his crown, and announced to the gathered magicians that they were to use whatever magic they had at their disposal to destroy the besieging forces.

"When?" someone called from the crowd.

"Right now," the king replied, smiling. He waved a dismissal, and retreated to his apartments.

The magicians looked at each other, shrugged, and began making magic, each after his or her own fashion.

The noted sorceress Rudhira the Red, for example, brewed up lightning in a kitchen cauldron, balls of crackling blue-white lightning that hissed and spattered sparks across the floor while they waited to be flung at a target.

The demonologist Kiramé of the Blue Hand etched a pentagram on an anteroom floor with blue chalk, and set about summoning a few cooperative demons.

A wizard named Kalthen the Fat found his way up the the battlements, where he began chanting a long, complicated spell intended to draw the floodwaters up from the river and wash the invaders away in a great wave.

Another wizard, Sancha the Foul, collected assorted leavings from the kitchen midden, sat down in the courtyard, and began assembling and animating homunculi, nasty little man-shaped creatures the size of your hand that he said would sneak out of the castle and torment the enemy with poisoned hatpins and whispered curses.

And all the various others set about their various fearsome magicks, while the poor little frog wizard just sat there in his corner, looking scared and nervous.

Amid all that terrible magic, it certainly looked as if King Bardec's army were doomed. The frog wizard saw no need to get involved.

But then things began to go wrong.

Kalthen's great wave swept up from the river just as Rudhira's lightnings spilled out of the castle, and the two collided with a great hissing roar; the water put out the fire, while the fire boiled the water away into steam, steam that drifted harmlessly up into the night sky.

Kiramé's demons sprang from the pentagram, hungry and ready for the sacrifice they had been promised. The invocation had directed them to devour all those who did not belong in the area, and they obeyed that—but instead of the enemy soldiers they snatched up Sancha's homunculi and gobbled them down like squirming candy. Homunculi didn't belong in the World at all, of course, and to a demon that was far more obvious than any human's nationality. Most demons, the legends of treachery notwithstanding, are not really very bright.

Their hunger satisfied, the demons then vanished, and could not safely be conjured again until the next time the greater moon was full.

Nor were these the only disasters as the magicians, accustomed to working in solitude, got in each other's way. Man-eating plants bloomed by moonlight and consumed witches rather than soldiers; spells of sudden death became entangled with spells designed to send the invaders dancing helplessly and harmlessly away, and sorcerers died in jigs and gavottes; fearful illusions overlapped each other in grotesque juxtapositions that caused more laughter than fear among the besiegers.

Demonologists were sent flying to the moons. Theurgists were swallowed by the earth. Spells backfired, misfired, and crossfired, and the castle filled with smoke and strange light, while unearthly howls echoed from the stone walls. The servants fled in terror, taking refuge in the cellars and towers, while the frog wizard cowered in the corner and waited for it all to be over.

Some of the spells worked properly—but not very many.

By dawn, the castle was still surrounded by about three hundred Lassuronian soldiers, and the magicians were all gone, banished or slain by spells gone wrong.

All, that is, except the frog wizard, who had stayed crouched in his corner, never even considering any attempt at magic.

As the sun rose, and the smoke cleared away, and the last eerie echoes faded, the castle's inhabitants crept out of hiding. The king, still in his regalia, emerged from his chamber and looked over the aftermath. His gaze swept across smeared pentagrams, spilled potions, and scattered scraps of wizards' robes, and fell at last on the frog wizard, curled up in the corner.

"You!" he called. "Come here!"

Reluctantly, the frog wizard got to his feet and came. He bowed deeply, and then knelt before the king.

"You're one of the magicians, aren't you?" King Kelder demanded.

The frog wizard nodded.

"You're a wizard?"

"Yes, your Majesty," the frog wizard replied.

"You can work real magic?" the king persisted.

"Yes, your Majesty," the frog wizard said, with only the slightest hesitation.

"Then *do* something about those soldiers out there!" King Kelder demanded.

"But, your Majesty…" the frog wizard began.

"*Do* something, wizard!" the king shouted.

The frog wizard had never liked being shouted at; it made it hard for him to think.

"*Do* something about those soldiers!" the king insisted, pointing out a nearby window and leaning over until he was yelling right in the wizard's face.

Without really meaning to, the frog wizard *did* something. He worked his one and only spell, directed at the soldiers outside, and all three hundred of them were abruptly transformed into frogs—very large, hungry bullfrogs, all rather startled by their sudden change.

At first nobody realized what had happened, and the king continued to shout for several minutes before somebody tugged at his sleeve and pointed out that the invaders were gone, and had been replaced by a horde of amphibians that were now hopping about in mad confusion.

The king stared out the window, and, forgetful of the royal dignity, most of the other people in the room crowded around him and peered out over his shoulders.

Sure enough, the invading army was gone.

King Kelder turned to the wizard and demanded, "Did you do that?"

The wizard, too miserable to speak at the thought of what he had done to all those men, merely nodded.

"Is it permanent?" the king asked.

The wizard nodded again.

"You're sure?"

"I'm afraid so, your Majesty," the wizard replied.

The king's face broke into a broad grin; he whooped with joy, and his crown fell from his head.

He caught it and tossed it in the air, then danced for joy in a manner not at all consonant with proper castle protocol, but quite understandable from a human point of view. After all, he had just been saved from certain death.

The wizard was nowhere near as happy, but he managed a weak smile in response to the king's obvious delight. And after all, he hadn't killed anyone, and for all he knew frogs could live long and happy lives, and soldiers faced death regularly as an occupational hazard. He tried to convince himself that it was all for the best.

In fact, it did seem to be all for the best, at least from the Mreghonian point of view. The war was clearly over, and had ended in an unmistakable Mreghonian victory.

The castle servants were sent out to investigate and to collect the spoils, and by sunset that day the royal armory was jammed to overflowing with captured weapons. The frogs had been chased away, scattering in all directions, and the entire army's supply train had thus been abandoned, completely intact, to the victors.

King Kelder and his councillors had spent the day alternately thinking up insulting terms to impose on King Bardec, if it should develop that he had not been among those transformed, and planning for a massive celebration of this miraculous deliverance.

The frog wizard sat in his corner, listening to all this, with no very clear idea what he was supposed to do other than feel guilty and miserable.

Nobody else seemed to think he had any reason to feel guilty and miserable, but *he* certainly thought so.

In all the excitement he was quite ignored, and both breakfast and lunch were somehow forgotten, so that around mid-afternoon he grew very hungry, so hungry that his stomach was making more noise than his conscience. Finally, he got up the nerve to approach the king and ask what was expected of him.

"Should I go home now?" he inquired.

"No, of course not!" the king replied. "You're my honored guest, at least until after the celebration!"

Servants were called, and the wizard was given a hearty meal and a pleasant room for the night, but he still didn't really know what to do with himself. All his books and belongings were still back in his cave, after all, and he didn't know anyone in the castle. He spent much of the time sitting on his bed thinking about all those poor frogs, or staring out the castle windows, or aimlessly wandering the castle corridors.

This went on for the three days it took to organize the victory celebration.

At the feast, the frog wizard was dragged out in front of the rowdy, half-drunk mob of peasants and petty nobles, and was declared the kingdom's Royal Magician. He was given the tallest tower in the castle for his own exclusive use, and servants were sent to his cave to fetch back all his belongings.

Everyone told the wizard that he was a hero. He tried very hard to feel like a hero, and to act like a hero, but he couldn't quite manage it. Failing that, he at least tried not to dampen anybody else's enthusiasm, and he had rather more success at this limited goal.

Indeed, everything in Mreghon seemed just fine for a time; the invading army was gone, and there were enough frogs to eat up all the extra flies and mosquitoes around the castle. The floods receded, the army returned to its usual duties, and life went on.

After awhile, though, unusual things began to happen.

Frogs began to turn up in odd places.

The weather was starting to turn colder, and ordinarily all the frogs would be burrowing down into pond-beds for the winter, but this year, instead, frogs were slipping into people's houses to stay warm. Peasants would come home from a day in the fields and find a couple of huge bullfrogs sitting on the hearth—big, determined bullfrogs that did not flee when chased with a fireplace poker, but merely ducked in a corner and waited for the poker-wielding peasant to give up and go away.

Frogs even began slipping into the castle.

And not only were these frogs getting in where they weren't wanted, but having consumed all the available insects, they were getting into the food, as well. Finding a frog on one's plate, licking at a pork chop or a leg of mutton, could ruin a man's appetite, and sent many a woman running for the poker.

Worst of all, the frogs seemed to recall enough of their human origins to have a rather warped sense of humor. Several people reported finding frogs in their beds and bathtubs, grinning lewdly—until now, nobody had realized that frogs *could* grin lewdly, but everyone agreed that that was exactly what the transformed Lassuronians did.

Even royalty was not spared. Queen Edara scandalized the castle by running out into the corridor shrieking and totally nude after discovering a frog crouched between her legs in the bath, grinning up at her and licking about lasciviously.

The last straw was when the king himself, while dispensing high justice in the throne room, realized that something was wrong. Everyone seemed to be staring at the top of his head.

Puzzled, he reached up and found a frog, perched atop his crown and leering over the gold and jewels at the gathered courtiers.

Furious, he flung the crown to the floor and charged from the room, his councillors at his heels. Shouting imprecations, he marched up the stairs to the castle's highest tower, where he barged into the wizard's chamber without knocking and demanded, "*Do* something about these damned frogs!"

The wizard, startled, looked up from the book he was reading, blinked, and said, "What?"

King Kelder turned an interesting shade of purple as he stood in the center of the wizard's chamber, speechless with fury, trying to think of something suitably scathing to say.

At last he burst out, "These damned frogs are all your fault! *You* turned those soldiers into frogs! You couldn't sweep them away with a whirlwind, or make the earth swallow them up, or turn them into something harmless like rocks or daisies, no, *you* had to turn them into *frogs*! And now we've got frogs coming out of our *ears*, frogs in the bath, frogs in our beds, frogs simply *everywhere*!"

At that moment, the frog that had been on the crown stuck its head out of the back of the king's collar, where it had fallen when the crown was snatched off, and croaked loudly.

The king could take no more; he began shrieking wordlessly at the wizard as his councillors watched in horror from the doorway.

The wizard simply sat on his bed, the book on his lap and a baffled expression on his face, trying to figure out what he was supposed to do.

At last, the king had to pause for breath, and the wizard asked mildly, "But what do you want me to *do*, your Majesty?"

"Do your damned *magic*, wizard! Do *something*!" the king said, as he marched forward and reached out to grab the wizard by the throat.

The wizard shrank back on the bed, but to no avail; King Kelder was a big man, and despite his age and his fat he had long, strong arms. He closed his hands around the wizard's neck and shouted, "*Do* something! *Do* something!"

The wizard had never liked being shouted at, and he discovered he liked being grabbed by the throat even less. It made thinking very difficult indeed.

So without any thinking, he *did* something. His hand came up in a magical gesture, and he *did* it.

He turned the King into a frog.

Instantly, as the hands shriveled away from his throat, he regretted it, but it was too late.

The councillors stared from the doorway as their sovereign shrank down inside his robes, turned green, and hopped out of his collar as a bullfrog.

This was no ordinary, placid frog, either. This was a big, fat frog, and this was a *very angry* frog. It let out a loud croak.

The other frog, the one that had been sitting at the back of the king's collar, croaked as well, and seemed to smirk.

The wizard looked at the two frogs, at the half-dozen courtiers jammed into his doorway, at the book on his lap, and then back at the two frogs sitting on the king's empty robes.

The situation, he saw, had gotten totally out of hand.

The wizard didn't think it would be a good idea to stay around. Not only would it not be a good idea to stay around for any extended period, but any stay *at all* seemed unwise.

In fact, he thought that the quickest possible departure would be a very good idea indeed. He hurriedly closed the book and put it aside, then got to his feet and raised a hand threateningly.

"Step aside," he said, "or I'll do the same to you!"

The king's councillors immediately stepped back, squeezing against both sides of the narrow hallway as the wizard marched past them and down the stairs.

Once he was out of sight he began running, because he knew that the councillors would not stay cowed for long. Sooner or later they would come after him, and the wizard did not want to know whether he really *would* turn more people into frogs if threatened with capture. He hoped he would not, but he wasn't sure.

He was safely across the drawbridge and out of the castle before he saw any signs of pursuit. Some simple little sleight-of-hand tricks sent most of the hunters off in the wrong direction, and he was able to slip safely away, across the border into Klathoa.

He made his way down to the highway, where he turned west and departed the Small Kingdoms for the Hegemony of Ethshar. By the middle of Newfrost he had reached the gates of Ethshar of the Spices itself.

In the city he found himself an honest, if humble, position as a scribe in the overlord's palace, copying out proclamations to be posted in the city's markets. He lived there in peace for the rest of his life, and he never again turned anyone into a frog.

Well…

Almost never.

ABOUT THE AUTHOR

Lawrence Watt-Evans is the author of four dozen novels and over a hundred short stories, including the Hugo-winning "Why I Left Harry's All-Night Hamburgers." He has been a full-time writer for more than thirty years and lives in Takoma Park, Maryland with his wife and an overweight cat.

His web page is at www.watt-evans.com, and readers of this book may also want to check out www.ethshar.com.

Made in the USA
Lexington, KY
10 February 2015